HEART OF DARKNESS

HEART OF DARKNESS

by Joseph Conrad

A Guide to Reading & Reflecting

Karen Swallow Prior

B&H
PUBLISHING
NASHVILLE, TENNESSEE

978-1-4627-9665-6

Published by B&H Publishing Group
Nashville Tennessee

Dewey Decimal Classification: 248.84
Subject Heading: ATTITUDE (PSYCHOLOGY) / CENTRAL
AFRICA / CHRISTIAN LIFE

Cover design and illustration by Ligia Teodosiu.

1 2 3 4 5 6 7 • 23 22 21 20

NOTE TO THE READER

The introduction is written to enlighten and
assist both those who have previously read
Heart of Darkness and those who have not.
In consideration of the latter, spoilers have
been avoided in the introduction so that
new readers may experience the delight of
surprise and discovery that all good books
hold. The introduction is intended to be a true
introduction to the work, one that will equip new
readers and returning ones with background
and knowledge that will increase understanding
and appreciation of the work without giving the
story away. The discussion questions at the end
of each section and at the end of the work are
designed for use after the novel has been read.

Footnotes are provided to define or explain most archaic words and usages. Some of the terms explained are repeated throughout the text, but they are defined only once, the first time they appear.

INTRODUCTION

About the Author

Józef Teodor Konrad Korzeniowski, who would later adopt the Anglicized pen name Joseph Conrad, was born December 3, 1857, in Russian-occupied Poland. Following his father's imprisonment for actions in support of Polish independence, the family was exiled to Siberia. Its cold climate eventually took a toll, and by the time Joseph, the only child, was eleven, both parents had died of tuberculosis, and Joseph was adopted by his mother's brother. Conrad's ability later in life to question colonization and its inherent cruelty was surely owed, at least in part, to this firsthand experience with political oppression and its devastating consequences in his own life.

Influenced by wide reading that included many stories of adventure and exploration, Conrad, while yet a youth, set his sights on a career at sea. Although he struggled with poor health and difficulty at school, Conrad (like his father, who had been a writer and translator) possessed a literary mind and a facility with languages. In addition to his native Polish, he became fluent in French, and later as an adult, learned English. These abilities assisted both his careers as a seaman and later as a writer.

Conrad's twenty-year career at sea began at age sixteen, when he went to France to begin work as a merchant marine. A few years later, burdened by gambling debts, Conrad attempted suicide by shooting himself in the chest, but, fortunately, survived. In 1878, in order to avoid being conscripted into the Russian military, he enlisted in the British merchant marine. Eight years later, he became a naturalized British subject and passed the examination to qualify as Master for the British Merchant Navy. In 1890, he took a position with a Belgian trading company as a steamboat captain on the Congo River. Conrad returned from that voyage sick in body from malaria—and sick in soul from what he witnessed in the Congo. This experience would be the basis for *Heart of Darkness*.

Conrad's life as a mariner took him all over the world. He began writing during his career at sea, using the people and places he encountered as sources. By 1894, beset with poor health and finding fewer openings on ships, he decided to leave the sea life to pursue writing full time, settling in England, where he would marry and father two children. When his first novel, *Almayer's Folly*, was published in 1895, he was thirty-eight years old and had been working on the book for several years. *Heart of Darkness* was his fourth published work, first printed in three serial installments in *Blackwood's Edinburgh Magazine* in 1899. He continued writing until his death (due to a heart attack) on August 3, 1924. During his life, he published thirty-one works (which included novels, plays, short stories, and essays) and wrote more than three thousand letters.

Conrad was deliberate and painstaking in his craft. He was a voracious reader, had studied the novel form, had befriended some of the most important literary figures of his age (including Rudyard Kipling, Ford Madox Ford, and John Galsworthy), and wrote, not in his first, or even second, but his third language. This choice required even greater deliberation and conscientiousness than necessary when communicating in one's mother tongue. It also helps explain the sometimes-laborious quality of his prose, as well as the distant, detached gloomy perspective typical of his narrators. Conrad struggled emotionally and mentally in composing his works. His letters are filled with confessions of fear, angst, and self-doubt. In one letter to his friend, the literary critic Edward Garnett (husband of Constance Garnett, famous translator of many classical literary works), Conrad asked Garnett if he had read Part 3 of *Heart of Darkness,* then expressed worry about his newest manuscript, confessing,

> The more I write the less substance do I see in my work. The scales are falling off my eyes. It is tolerably awful. And I face it, I face it but the fright is growing on me. My fortitude is shaken by the view of the monster. It does not move; its eyes are baleful; it is as still as death itself—and it will devour me. Its stare has eaten into

my soul already deep, deep. I am alone
with it in a chasm with perpendicular
sides of black basalt. Never were sides so
perpendicular and smooth, and high.[1]

Either Conrad's natural constitution or his
difficult life experiences alone could provide
sufficient explanation for his dark outlook. But
the combination of these factors—amplified
further perhaps by the lack of a devout religious
faith—makes such a perspective seem inevitable.
Like most Poles of his time, Conrad was born
into a Catholic family. While he never formally
renounced religion, skepticism and doubt were his
assumed posture, as they were for many in the
literary and intellectual circles of his time. In a
1908 letter to Garnett, Conrad wrote, half-jokingly,
"I wish I could believe in an intelligent, benevolent
Supreme Being to whom I could leave the task of
paying my debts such debts as the one I owe you
for instance. And perhaps there is one. I don't
know . . ."[2]

Yet, as brutal as the world of *Heart of Darkness*
is, it is not a world in which God is absent in the

---

[1] https://archive.org/stream/lettersfromjosep007757mbp/
lettersfromjosep007757mbp_djvu.txt

[2] Ibid.

same way He is absent in the works of some of
Conrad's literary contemporaries. In the novels
of Thomas Hardy, for example, religious belief
is treated, at best, as superstition or, at worst,
the cause of evil. In contrast to Hardy's cold,
intellectual disavowal of God, *Heart of Darkness* is,
in some ways, an implicit acknowledgment of the
human need of something bigger than and outside
ourselves to check our basest human impulses
and most craven tendencies. Conrad's lament over
darkness expresses a desire for the light.

Background of the Work

Although it is a work of fiction, *Heart of
Darkness* is deeply rooted in both biographical
and historical facts. In writing the novel, Conrad
drew upon the diary he kept of his own voyage on
the Congo as the employee of a Belgian trading
company. A good deal of literary criticism on
Conrad and his fiction has examined just how
closely Conrad's fictional narrator, Marlow (who
appears in other of Conrad's works), aligns with
Conrad's own experiences and views. Certainly,
there is a great deal of overlap, but in the end,
Conrad was an artist; his fictional works are

works of art that reveal truths about the human condition.

The setting of the primary action in *Heart of Darkness* is what is today called the Democratic Republic of the Congo (formerly Zaire). From 1885 to 1908, 900,000 square miles of central Africa were controlled by Belgium's King Leopold II. Leopold called his territory Congo Free State (a tragically ironic name). Although a corporate state, the territory functioned, essentially, as the world's largest private plantation. Though Leopold never set foot on its land, by exploiting tribal rivalries and unwitting (as well as not so unwitting) European traders, he operated a reign of terror that wiped out, by some estimates, half of the native population. Native workers who failed to be sufficiently productive had their hands or feet cut off, or sometimes, in order to preserve their ability to continue to work, the hands and feet of their children were butchered instead. Men were chained, whipped, and executed at will. Women were raped, and entire villages burned. The deplorable treatment of the natives described in *Heart of Darkness* reflects real events that Conrad witnessed during a period that lasted long enough and were recent enough that some of these atrocities are documented in black and white photographs.

These events occurred during a period known as the New Imperialism. During the late nineteenth and early twentieth centuries, European powers expanded colonization efforts in territories across the world, particularly in Africa. Sadly, Christianity played a central role in these exploits. Imperialism was often promoted and justified as a missionary endeavor with the aim of bringing Christianity and "civilization" to foreign lands (as conveyed in *Heart of Darkness*). For example, Henry Stanley—most famous for locating the long-missing Scottish missionary and greeting him, allegedly, with the legendary words, "Dr. Livingstone, I presume"—was enlisted by King Leopold, in the name of Christian missions, to build the infrastructure in the Congo, thereby assisting Leopold in his hold over the land and its people.

In *Heart of Darkness*, Conrad takes pains to transform this very particular historical and geographical context into a more universalized story. Though based on his real-life experiences, the "Company" as well as most of the places and people in the story are unnamed. Even the jungle and the river itself seem more like scenes from myths and legends—or even our own nightmares—than any actual place on the world map. In this way, *Heart of Darkness* is as much about larger philosophical ideas, political impulses, and the human condition as it is about historical events. One emerging philosophy at work in *Heart of Darkness* is existentialism, an idea that gained traction in the later nineteenth and early twentieth centuries. Although it takes various forms, existentialism grapples with what it means for human beings to exist apart from the sort of pre-determined purpose or meaning that comes from outside oneself (such as from God). Existentialism acknowledges that if (as the madman in the existentialist philosopher Friedrich Nietzsche's work *The Gay Science* exclaimed) "God is dead," so too are reason, logic, and order because these, too, ultimately come from outside ourselves. If such larger foundations of reality can no longer be assumed, it is necessary for humans to create for themselves the meaning of their existence. Indeed, within the terms set by existentialism, it becomes the human being's greatest responsibility to forge an authentic meaning for one's life because—apart from an eternal absolute source of meaning—human existence is absurd. The word *absurd* literally means lacking reason or order;

unsound—a concept that is central to *Heart of Darkness*. Within existentialism, exercising one's moral agency, or choice, becomes the highest expression of humanity. *Heart of Darkness*, written in the midst of the ascendancy of these ideas, is preoccupied with this search for meaning. If life is ultimately meaningless, then at best what it offers, as Marlow says in the text, is "a choice of nightmares."

Form of the Work

The heavy subject matter of *Heart of Darkness* is not the only quality that makes it a difficult work to read. Conrad's writing is highly crafted and precise—yet, at the same time, is as dense and meandering as the jungle itself. In his preface to a later novel, *The Nigger of the "Narcissus,"* Conrad explains his view of art and of writing in general, describing words as a means of revealing truth about the world in the same way an artist uses paint to do the same:

> A work that aspires, however humbly,
> to the condition of art should carry its
> justification in every line. And art itself
> may be defined as a single-minded

attempt to render the highest kind of
justice to the visible universe, by bringing
to light the truth, manifold and one,
underlying its every aspect.

In "carrying its justification in every line,"
Heart of Darkness is best read almost as if it were
a poem—slowly, with attention and appreciation
for the significance suggested by repetition, the
lushness of the language, and the rich resonances
that language suggests. Like a poem, *Heart of
Darkness* is laden with imagery that conveys
far more than the events of the narrative alone.
One powerful example of the poetic language is
seen when Marlow says, evocatively, that during
his voyage on the Congo, "The earth seemed
unearthly." These four simple words convey far
more than might be communicated in ten times as
many.

Before anything happens or anyone speaks
within the narrative, the opening paragraphs
establish an elegiac and ethereal tone, one that
carries through the entire book, conveyed through
words such as *flutter, at rest, vanishing, motionless,
mournful, brooding,* and *gloom.* This imagery of
death foreshadows the literal deaths that will
occur later in the story. These images also hint at

the overall meaning of Marlow's experience: "And for a moment it seemed to me as if I also were buried in a vast grave full of unspeakable secrets . . . intolerable weight oppressing my breast, the damp earth, the unseen presence of victorious corruption, the darkness of an impenetrable night."

In addition to its poetic language, the larger formal aspects of the work also contribute to the complexities of its meaning. First, even the genre or literary category *Heart of Darkness* fits into is ambiguous. The work's odd length, combined into three neat parts, presents a form that defies the major traditional genres of literature. It is most properly categorized as a novella, but is sometimes referred to as a short story (a long one) or a novel (a short one). Second, *Heart of Darkness* is a frame narrative, a story that is surrounded or framed by an outer story. A frame narrative is a bit like the children's game of telephone in which, by the end of the round, the original message has been altered significantly (sometimes beyond recognition) by the tellers. While, of course, in a literary work the author is in control of each narrator's words, the authorial choice of layering perspective on perspective reinforces the limitations of each person's point of view. Such

a technique is a dramatic departure from the
omniscient narrators of earlier nineteenth-century
novelists such as Charles Dickens and William
Makepeace Thackeray.

While most of the narrative in *Heart of
Darkness* consists of Marlow's story, he is not the
initial narrator. Rather, the unnamed first-person
narrator of the entire work, the frame narrator,
is one of the group of five men sitting on the
anchored yacht. Marlow is one member of this
group. The story Marlow tells the others while they
wait comprises most of the narrative. Occasional
breaks in Marlow's narrative remind the reader
of the scene in which he is telling his story. The
frame around the narrative is so thin that it might
be tempting to think it makes no difference. One
way to think about the difference this technique
does make is to ask how the story and its overall
effect would be changed without the additional
narrative layer. Other famous examples of frame
narrative—such as *Frankenstein, Wuthering
Heights, The Turn of the Screw,* and *The Rime of
the Ancient Mariner*—show that the presence of the
frame contributes significantly to the story's effect
and meaning overall, as it does here.

Like the mariner in Coleridge's *Rime of the
Ancient Mariner,* Marlow is burdened with the task

of telling his story in order to fulfill its meaning. Yet Marlow's narrative differs from the ancient mariner's in that the meaning of his experience still seems to him to be undetermined (or *inscrutable*, a word that appears several times in the text). The frame narrator states, in fact, that for Marlow the meaning of a story is to be found not inside but outside, constructed rather than discovered:

> The yarns of seamen have a direct simplicity, the whole meaning of which lies within the shell of a cracked nut. But Marlow was not typical (if his propensity to spin yarns be excepted), and to him the meaning of an episode was not inside like a kernel but outside, enveloping the tale which brought it out only as a glow brings out a haze, in the likeness of one of these misty halos that sometimes are made visible by the spectral illumination of moonshine.

Such indeterminacy is one way in which *Heart of Darkness* points toward the modernist movement it preceded. Modernism is a movement of art and literature of the early twentieth century that challenged traditional authority, forms, and mores. It was, largely, a reaction against the religion, morality, and optimism of the Victorian age and the excesses of late imperialism. But the movement was also a natural response to the devastation wrought by industrialization, humanistic philosophies, and World War I. Modernism didn't so much reject the notion of truth (that would come later) as it emphasized that truth can be seen only in part. The modernist movement emphasizes perspective, both its power and its limitations, as exemplified by the impressionist, expressionist, and cubist art to which modernism gave birth.

This idea underlying modernist epistemology— that truth can be known only through a multiplicity of perspectives—is central to the frame narrative of *Heart of Darkness*. The outer frame is the thin, but essential, outside perspective of the unnamed narrator whose words frame Marlow's words, which, in turn, frame the words of Kurtz at the heart of the story. This layering of various limited perspectives calls attention to what can be known and what cannot, to the blurred distinctions between reality, dream, and nightmare. As Marlow tells his auditors on the yacht,

"No, it is impossible; it is impossible to
convey the life-sensation of any given
epoch of one's existence—that which
makes its truth, its meaning—its subtle
and penetrating essence. It is impossible.
We live, as we dream—alone."

Yet, while its modernist epistemology keenly
predicts the age ahead, *Heart of Darkness* also
reflects the ethos of the late Victorian era in
which it was written. Fueled by the Industrial
Revolution and the economic prosperity it brought,
the Victorian age (1837–1901) was characterized
by the spirits of industry, exploration, optimism,
and progress. By the end of the age, however,
the sinister side of each of these good things
began to emerge. Thus, in *Heart of Darkness*, the
once-promising machines are found broken and
decaying, the potential proselytes have become
slaves, the exported goods are extracted at great
moral cost, and the enlightened Europeans have
exchanged civilization for animalism. These
darker realities reflect ideas and perspectives that
gained traction in the latter half of the Victorian
age, including Charles Darwin's theory of the
survival of the fittest, Sigmund Freud's theory of
the subconscious mind, and Friedrich Nietzsche's

will to power. Like these philosophies, *Heart of Darkness* raises questions about the traditions of the age, but unlike the later modernists (such as James Joyce and Virginia Woolf), Conrad does not outright reject such traditions. *Heart of Darkness* recognizes, as does Marlow once he discovers the grounded steam ship, that without rivets to hold things together, nothing works.

Themes of the Work

As with any work of great literature, it becomes impossible, at some point, to separate the form of the work from its themes or meaning. Meaning proceeds from the form. One of *Heart of Darkness*'s major themes—the nature of truth— is demonstrated powerfully, as already seen, through the very form of the frame narrative. But truth is also explicitly addressed through the events of the story. Conrad was concerned with truth—he believed in it—as shown in a letter he wrote in 1897: "And suppose Truth is just around the corner like the elusive and useless loafer it is? I can't tell. No one can tell. It is impossible to know anything tho' it is possible to believe a thing or two."[3] For Conrad, story was a way to get at elusive truth. In a 1905 essay he wrote about fellow novelist Henry James, Conrad explains his view that fiction gets at the truth of human experience better than history does:

> Fiction is history, human history, or it is nothing. But it is also more than that; it stands on firmer ground, being based on the reality of forms and the observation of social phenomena, whereas history is based on documents, and the reading of print and handwriting—on second-hand impression. Thus fiction is nearer truth.[4]

Although *Heart of Darkness* emphasizes the complexity of truth, it does not (as later movements in art and culture would do) dismiss its existence altogether. Marlow (who is neither entirely reliable nor who can be assumed to represent Conrad's view) claims to be an advocate for truth, declaring, "You know I hate, detest, and can't bear a lie, not because I am straighter than

---

[3] *The Collected Letters of Joseph Conrad*, eds. Frederick Karl and Laurence Davies (Cambridge: Cambridge University Press, 1983), 370.

[4] "Henry James—An Appreciation," 1905; https://ebooks .adelaide.edu.au/c/conrad/joseph/c75nl/chapter2.html.

the rest of us, but simply because it appalls me. There is a taint of death, a flavor of mortality in lies—which is exactly what I hate and detest in the world—what I want to forget. It makes me miserable and sick, like biting something rotten would do." Yet, the story ends in a way that calls this declaration into question, asking the reader to consider not only the nature of truth and how we know it, but also what we do with that truth once we have seen it. The novel also asks the reader what to do with a liar who can't bear a lie.

A second major theme of the work is captured in the title itself. On the surface, the title phrase refers to the long, arduous journey into the center of the mysterious Congo. The story also makes many references to the assumption of Conrad's world that European civilization is associated with light (particularly, the Enlightenment) while Africa and other non-Western cultures have yet to be enlightened. However, a more significant meaning emerges as Marlow comes face-to-face with a truth he has seen glimpses of all along: the heart of human beings—absent any restraints, whether internal or external—is horrifyingly dark. The motif of restraint, repeated throughout the story, was (like duty and earnestness) a central value of the Victorian era. But by the end of the age,

questions about the limits of restraint were being
raised. What Marlow encounters in the *Heart of
Darkness* exposes what happens to—and at the
hands of—humans when all restraints are thrown
off.

Much of the power of the story hinges on the
assumption of Conrad's world (and our own,
too, though it is expressed less explicitly today)
that Europe represents "civilization" and Africa
"savagery" (the titular "heart of darkness"). This
is the assumption Marlow takes with him into the
Congo and the one held by Conrad's contemporary
readers. But everything that happens in the story
reveals that assumption to be a lie. In contrast
to the Enlightenment's seeming promise of
progress, what is revealed in *Heart of Darkness*
is regress. The great paradox of the story is
that the "civilized" Europeans are, in fact, most
uncivilized. Even that prime symbol of the age of
progress—the machine—is rendered useless here
as the image of the "railway-truck lying there on
its back with its wheels in the air" that Conrad
encounters upon his arrival at the company
station suggests. The Europeans Marlow meets
who are working for the Belgian trade company
in the Congo offer troubling portrayals of how
"civilization" is merely a thin veneer covering deep

human depravity. Except for Kurtz and Marlow, the company's employees are unnamed, identified by their occupations alone. This is a telling sign of their one-dimensional nature and how their material aspirations have robbed them of their inner humanity.

The first company man that Marlow meets is the chief accountant. Following a lengthy, horrific description of the shackled African slaves Marlow finds laboring, starving, and dying in the heat, the accountant appears on the scene, wearing "a high-starched collar, white cuffs . . . snowy trousers . . . and varnished boots." The contrast is meant to shock, and it does. Then, after continuing his trek, Marlow meets the bricklayer and the company manager at the Central Station. Marlow calls the bricklayer, with "a little forked beard and a hooked nose," a "*papier-mâché* Mephistopheles," one of the most devastating descriptions in the book: he is a completely soulless devil. The bricklayer has been at the station for more than a year, doing nothing but uselessly waiting for materials with which to make bricks. The manager is non-descript except that his eyes, "of the usual blue," are "perhaps remarkably cold." And the expression of his lips ("something stealthy—a smile—not a smile . . . a seal applied on the words to make the meaning of the commonest phrase appear inscrutable") is terrifying, a perfect embodiment—in the words made famous by the twentieth-century philosopher Hannah Arendt—of "the banality of evil." The manager "inspired uneasiness," Marlowe says. "He was great by this little thing that it was impossible to tell what could control such a man. He never gave that secret away. Perhaps there was nothing within him." The hollowness of all of these characters inspired T. S. Eliot's poem, "The Hollow Men," which includes in its epigraph one of the famous lines from *Heart of Darkness*.

Such men were empowered, in part, by the rationalization of the Christian mission of bringing the gospel and "civilization" to pagan lands. Conrad captures the common but naïve belief that colonization was a gospel effort early in *Heart of Darkness* when Marlow recounts his aunt's perspective as he prepared to depart for Africa. She saw him, he says, as:

> Something like an emissary of light, something like a lower sort of apostle. There had been a lot of such rot let loose in print and talk just about that time, and the excellent woman, living right in the rush of all that humbug, got carried off

her feet. She talked about "weaning those ignorant millions from their horrid ways," till, upon my word, she made me quite uncomfortable. I ventured to hint that the Company was run for profit.

Later, referring to the expedition's agents as "pilgrims," Marlow points to a deep irony in such great evil being done in the name of Christianity. The workers who accompany Marlow on his quest to find the missing Kurtz are indeed on a kind of pilgrimage. But it is a pilgrimage that is far from holy—a point foreshadowed early in the narrative when Marlow stumbles upon "the body of a middle-aged Negro, with a bullet-hole in the forehead" along a path. Rather than anything remotely resembling the gospel or even civilization, what these pilgrims and their employers bring are death and destruction.

Reading *Heart of Darkness* as a Christian Today

Heart of Darkness is, notoriously, not a fun or pleasant read. But it is an important one. Conrad's worldview reflects a distant longing for God, but no real knowledge of or proximity to that God. Yet, as all great literature does, *Heart of Darkness* reveals qualities that are central to our common humanity, regardless of our tribe or tongue. Among these are our need for restraint from our own greed and lusts and our desire to worship someone or something other than God—or even to be worshipped.

Because it is such a complicated text, a number of problems of interpretation surround *Heart of Darkness*. The sheer ambiguity of the story's meaning is the source of many interpretive difficulties. To read the work is to witness a conscience in conflict, two consciences, in fact: Conrad's and Marlow's. As the literary critic Edward Said has noted, it was difficult if not impossible for Conrad to see past his own imperialistic Eurocentric worldview far enough to imagine something outside it, even as he saw enough to critique it. Thus, Marlow's views of the African natives largely reflect the racist views of the colonizing Europeans. Yet, when Marlow says that "all Europe contributed to the making of Kurtz" (one of the brilliantly ambiguous moments in the book) he refers, in part, to those qualities that reflect Kurtz's great giftedness and the way that giftedness contributed to the evils to which he succumbed. Marlow seems to simultaneously acknowledge and resist the notion that it is possible to know and practice truth, and to distinguish between good and evil. Indeed, ambiguity itself is a theme of the work, both moral and textual ambiguity. This is what makes *Heart of Darkness* such a great work—and what renders it frustrating for many readers.

To postcolonial readers of today, the text looks more complicit in the imperialist mind-set than it did to its contemporary readers and critics, who largely took it as an attack on European colonial methods. Today the prominent place of the work within the literary canon has been called into question by new understandings brought to light by the postcolonial era. Some of the most controversial critical questions concern the extent to which the text is racist (by both the standards of its own time and ours) and how closely Conrad's views align with those of Marlow. Addressing this question requires distinguishing between imperialism and racism, as well as seeing how closely the two have historically been connected.

In the nineteenth century, the British Empire was an empire like the world had never seen. The leading world power at this time, the small island expanded its power to territories that eventually covered one-quarter of the globe. British colonization was fueled by various ideologies and interests, including those related to trade and commerce. However, racism was foundational. The inextricable link between racism and imperialism is immortalized in Rudyard Kipling's poem, "The White Man's Burden," published (in the same year as *Heart of Darkness*) to encourage the United States to expand its territory into the Philippines. Some of the poem's most famous lines are these, addressed to the "white man":

> Send forth the best ye breed—
> Go send your sons to exile
> To serve your captives' need
> To wait in heavy harness
> On fluttered folk and wild—
> Your new-caught, sullen peoples,
> Half devil and half child.

Like this poem, *Heart of Darkness* contains language and ideas that should make modern readers uncomfortable in their explicit and implicit dehumanization of people. In wrestling with this discomfort, it is essential to distinguish between racism and prejudice, terms often used interchangeably. Prejudice is simply a preconceived idea not based on actual knowledge or experience (something impossible for any thinking human to avoid entirely). Racism is the belief that one race is superior to another (or can refer to behaviors and systems rooted in such belief). Despite the moments in which he seems to wrestle with his preconceived notions or prejudices, Marlow's racism runs deeper and needs to be considered separately.

The racist assumptions of nineteenth-century Europe are also questioned by the work. For example, Marlow acknowledges—insists, even—that African people, whose behavior and language are so strange to him, are "not inhuman." He also recognizes the evil of slavery when he says that the slave drivers "were strong, lusty, red-eyed devils, that swayed and drove men—men, I tell you." Associating the Europeans with the demonic reverses a common imperialistic trope in a remarkable way, revealing Conrad's questioning of received European notions. And in one of the most famous lines from the book, Marlow observes, "The conquest of the earth, which mostly means the taking it away from those who have a different complexion or slightly flatter noses than ourselves, is not a pretty thing when you look into it too much."

This recognition is, of course insufficient in itself. One can believe in the humanity of another race without believing the races are equal. The

Nigerian novelist Chinua Achebe says that some of the passages some readers might consider to demonstrate Conrad's kindness toward the African people, in fact, "constitute his best assaults." In a 1975 lecture that has become a centerpiece within postcolonial literary criticism, Achebe distinguished between imperialism and racism, arguing that Conrad rejected the former while being blind to the latter. Because of its racism, Achebe questioned the high place *Heart of Darkness* has held in the Western literary canon, going on even to criticize its literary merits, saying that Conrad's style causes a "hypnotic stupor in his readers through a bombardment of emotive words."[5] Achebe's view is an important one to consider in reading *Heart of Darkness.* It is also helpful to read Achebe's own novel, *Things Fall Apart*, alongside *Heart of Darkness* in order to see colonization from the viewpoint of the colonized rather than the colonizer.

Racism was only one reason it was difficult for nineteenth-century Europeans to see past their imperialist worldview. Another reason was that colonizing efforts were cloaked in the

---

[5] https://polonistyka.amu.edu.pl/__data/assets/pdf_file/0007/259954/Chinua-Achebe,-An-Image-of-Africa.-Racism-in-Conrads-Heart-of-Darkness.pdf

language of Christianity. The late eighteenth and early nineteenth centuries saw an explosion of missionary societies as a result of the evangelical revival that began in the 1730s under the leadership of John and Charles Wesley and George Whitefield. Imperialism and evangelism were so inextricably connected that nineteenth- (and even twentieth-) century missions could hardly be conceived of apart from colonizing.

Whatever good could be achieved by bringing ideas, resources, and the gospel to other countries was diminished when accompanied (as it often was) by what is now called the "white savior complex," a term that describes the way even well-intentioned Christians often sought to "rescue" native peoples rather than to equip and empower them and their communities. This mind-set is captured perfectly in the poem "The White Man's Burden," quoted from above, which presents imperialism as a service, a sacrifice even, that is the duty of white men toward the "wild" and "sullen" people of other lands. Thus, for the Christian, reading *Heart of Darkness* offers a necessary, if painful, glimpse of the dark side of the spirit of conquest that has characterized Christianity through too much of its history.

Another blind spot of the age that *Heart of Darkness* exposes (one the text seems to question even less than imperialism and racism) is sexism. The story is one centered on the world of men, of course. There are female characters in the story. They play important roles, but in subtle ways that ultimately serve what happens to the men. Moreover, the women are often treated dismissively. For example, in reference to his aunt, noted above for her naïve view of what Marlow and his company were doing in the Congo, Marlow says, "It's queer how out of touch with truth women are. They live in a world of their own . . ." This contemptuous attitude toward women culminates in the final scene when Marlow calls upon Kurtz's Intended. Other women in the story fulfill mythical or stereotypical roles, including Kurtz's African mistress and the two women knitting black wool inside the company's offices, "guarding the door of Darkness," like the Fates of Greek myth who weave the future.

While the novel's treatment of women can be viewed as rooted in sexism, the overwhelming sense of the novel is more misanthropic, that is, pessimistic about human beings and the human condition overall, regardless of sex. The world

portrayed in the novel is unkind to men and
women alike.

Much of what is startling in the story to readers
today are ideas and attitudes that were merely
assumed at the time. The shock felt today can
serve as a reminder that every age has its blind
spots, and that Christians are not immune from
these. The late Victorian Christians of Conrad's
age could not always see the difference between
cultural values and biblical principles. The same
is true of believers of every age, including our
own. Evangelicalism was such an influential
force shaping the Victorian age that even today's
American evangelical subculture often confuses
Victorian values for biblical ones. A careful reading
of *Heart of Darkness* can help Christians to
disentangle the two and, in so doing, separate the
wheat from the chaff of the work's racism, sexism,
and worldly philosophies. The task of the Christian
reader is to see the particulars found in the
context of the work and its author and to measure
them against both the standards of that time and
the standards of unchanging, universal biblical
truth. While some readers might be tempted to see
the moral and epistemological ambiguities the text
wrestles with as affirmation of the idea that there
is no such thing as truth, more careful readers

will see that the weight of these questions consists in the assumption that there is, in fact, moral truth: right and wrong, good and evil. We recognize darkness only because there is light.

I

The Nellie, a cruising yawl,[1] swung to her anchor without a flutter of the sails, and was at rest. The flood had made, the wind was nearly calm, and being bound down the river, the only thing for it was to come to and wait for the turn of the tide.

The sea-reach of the Thames[2] stretched before us like the beginning of an interminable waterway. In the offing[3] the sea and the sky

---

[1] A type of sailboat
[2] England's longest river, flowing through London and emptying into the North Sea
[3] The deep sea visible from the shore

were welded together without a joint, and in the luminous space the tanned sails of the barges drifting up with the tide seemed to stand still in red clusters of canvas sharply peaked, with gleams of varnished sprits. A haze rested on the low shores that ran out to sea in vanishing flatness. The air was dark above Gravesend,[4] and farther back still seemed condensed into a mournful gloom, brooding motionless over the biggest, and the greatest, town on earth.

The Director of Companies was our captain and our host. We four affectionately watched his back as he stood in the bows looking to seaward. On the whole river there was nothing that looked half so nautical. He resembled a pilot, which to a seaman is trustworthiness personified. It was difficult to realize his work was not out there in the luminous estuary, but behind him, within the brooding gloom.

Between us there was, as I have already said somewhere, the bond of the sea. Besides holding our hearts together through long periods of separation, it had the effect of making us tolerant of each other's yarns—and even convictions. The Lawyer—the best of old fellows—had, because

---

[4] An ancient town southeast of London

of his many years and many virtues, the only cushion on deck, and was lying on the only rug. The Accountant had brought out already a box of dominoes, and was toying architecturally with the bones.[5] Marlow sat cross-legged right aft, leaning against the mizzen-mast. He had sunken cheeks, a yellow complexion, a straight back, an ascetic aspect, and, with his arms dropped, the palms of hands outwards, resembled an idol. The director, satisfied the anchor had good hold, made his way aft and sat down amongst us. We exchanged a few words lazily. Afterwards there was silence on board the yacht. For some reason or other we did not begin that game of dominoes. We felt meditative, and fit for nothing but placid staring. The day was ending in a serenity of still and exquisite brilliance. The water shone pacifically; the sky, without a speck, was a benign immensity of unstained light; the very mist on the Essex marsh was like a gauzy and radiant fabric, hung from the wooded rises inland, and draping the low shores in diaphanous folds. Only the gloom to the west, brooding over the upper reaches, became more somber every minute, as if angered by the approach of the sun.

---

[5] Dominoes were sometimes made from ivory and therefore called "bones."

And at last, in its curved and imperceptible fall, the sun sank low, and from glowing white changed to a dull red without rays and without heat, as if about to go out suddenly, stricken to death by the touch of that gloom brooding over a crowd of men.

Forthwith a change came over the waters, and the serenity became less brilliant but more profound. The old river in its broad reach rested unruffled at the decline of day, after ages of good service done to the race that peopled its banks, spread out in the tranquil dignity of a waterway leading to the uttermost ends of the earth. We looked at the venerable stream not in the vivid flush of a short day that comes and departs forever, but in the august light of abiding memories. And indeed nothing is easier for a man who has, as the phrase goes, "followed the sea" with reverence and affection, than to evoke the great spirit of the past upon the lower reaches of the Thames. The tidal current runs to and fro in its unceasing service, crowded with memories of men and ships it had borne to the rest of home or to the battles of the sea. It had known and served all the men of whom the nation is proud, from Sir Francis Drake to Sir John Franklin, knights all, titled and untitled—the great knights-errant of the sea. It had borne all the ships whose

names are like jewels flashing in the night of
time, from the *Golden Hind* returning with her
round flanks full of treasure, to be visited by
the Queen's Highness and thus pass out of the
gigantic tale, to the *Erebus* and *Terror*, bound on
other conquests—and that never returned. It had
known the ships and the men. They had sailed
from Deptford, from Greenwich, from Erith—the
adventurers and the settlers; kings' ships and
the ships of men on 'Change;[6] captains, admirals,
the dark "interlopers"[7] of the Eastern trade, and
the commissioned "generals" of East India fleets.
Hunters for gold or pursuers of fame, they all had
gone out on that stream, bearing the sword, and
often the torch, messengers of the might within
the land, bearers of a spark from the sacred fire.
What greatness had not floated on the ebb of that
river into the mystery of an unknown earth! . . .
The dreams of men, the seed of commonwealths,
the germs of empires.

The sun set; the dusk fell on the stream,
and lights began to appear along the shore. The
Chapman light-house, a three-legged thing erect
on a mud-flat, shone strongly. Lights of ships

---

[6] Merchants
[7] Ships run by private traders

moved in the fairway—a great stir of lights going up and going down. And farther west on the upper reaches the place of the monstrous town was still marked ominously on the sky, a brooding gloom in sunshine, a lurid glare under the stars.

"And this also," said Marlow suddenly, "has been one of the dark places of the earth."

He was the only man of us who still "followed the sea." The worst that could be said of him was that he did not represent his class. He was a seaman, but he was a wanderer, too, while most seamen lead, if one may so express it, a sedentary life. Their minds are of the stay-at-home order, and their home is always with them—the ship; and so is their country—the sea. One ship is very much like another, and the sea is always the same. In the immutability of their surroundings the foreign shores, the foreign faces, the changing immensity of life, glide past, veiled not by a sense of mystery but by a slightly disdainful ignorance; for there is nothing mysterious to a seaman unless it be the sea itself, which is the mistress of his existence and as inscrutable as Destiny. For the rest, after his hours of work, a casual stroll or a casual spree on shore suffices to unfold for him the secret of a whole continent, and generally he finds the secret not worth knowing. The yarns

of seamen have an effective simplicity, the whole
meaning of which lies within the shell of a cracked
nut. But, as has been said, Marlow was not typical
(if his propensity to spin yarns be excepted), and
to him the meaning of an episode was not inside
like a kernel but outside, enveloping the tale
which brought it out only as a glow brings out a
haze, in the likeness of one of these misty halos
that sometimes are made visible by the spectral
illumination of moonshine.

His remark did not seem at all surprising. It
was just like Marlow. It was accepted in silence. No
one took the trouble to grunt even; and presently
he said, very slow—"I was thinking of very old
times, when the Romans first came here, nineteen
hundred years ago—the other day. . . . Light came
out of this river since—you say Knights? Yes; but
it is like a running blaze on a plain, like a flash of
lightning in the clouds. We live in the flicker—may
it last as long as the old earth keeps rolling! But
darkness was here yesterday. Imagine the feelings
of a commander of a fine—what d'ye call 'em?—
trireme[8] in the Mediterranean, ordered suddenly
to the north; run overland across the Gauls in

---

[8] An ancient type of sea vessel operated by oarsmen (often
slaves)

a hurry; put in charge of one of these craft the legionaries—a wonderful lot of handy men they must have been, too—used to build, apparently by the hundred, in a month or two, if we may believe what we read. Imagine him here—the very end of the world, a sea the colour of lead, a sky the colour of smoke, a kind of ship about as rigid as a concertina—and going up this river with stores, or orders, or what you like. Sand-banks, marshes, forests, savages,—precious little to eat fit for a civilized man, nothing but Thames water to drink. No Falernian wine[9] here, no going ashore. Here and there a military camp lost in a wilderness, like a needle in a bundle of hay—cold, fog, tempests, disease, exile, and death—death skulking in the air, in the water, in the bush. They must have been dying like flies here. Oh, yes—he did it. Did it very well, too, no doubt, and without thinking much about it either, except afterwards to brag of what he had gone through in his time, perhaps. They were men enough to face the darkness. And perhaps he was cheered by keeping his eye on a chance of promotion to the fleet at Ravenna[10] by and by, if he had good friends in Rome and

---

[9] A strong wine famous among ancient Roman writers
[10] Roman naval base

survived the awful climate. Or think of a decent
young citizen in a toga—perhaps too much dice,
you know—coming out here in the train of some
prefect, or tax-gatherer, or trader even, to mend
his fortunes. Land in a swamp, march through the
woods, and in some inland post feel the savagery,
the utter savagery, had closed round him—all that
mysterious life of the wilderness that stirs in the
forests, in the jungles, in the hearts of wild men.
There's no initiation either into such mysteries. He
has to live in the midst of the incomprehensible,
which is also detestable. And it has a fascination,
too, that goes to work upon him. The fascination of
the abomination—you know, imagine the growing
regrets, the longing to escape, the powerless
disgust, the surrender, the hate."

He paused.

"Mind," he began again, lifting one arm from
the elbow, the palm of the hand outwards, so that,
with his legs folded before him, he had the pose
of a Buddha preaching in European clothes and
without a lotus-flower—"Mind, none of us would
feel exactly like this. What saves us is efficiency—
the devotion to efficiency. But these chaps were
not much account, really. They were no colonists;
their administration was merely a squeeze, and
nothing more, I suspect. They were conquerors,

and for that you want only brute force—nothing
to boast of, when you have it, since your strength
is just an accident arising from the weakness of
others. They grabbed what they could get for the
sake of what was to be got. It was just robbery
with violence, aggravated murder on a great scale,
and men going at it blind—as is very proper for
those who tackle a darkness. The conquest of the
earth, which mostly means the taking it away from
those who have a different complexion or slightly
flatter noses than ourselves, is not a pretty thing
when you look into it too much. What redeems it
is the idea only. An idea at the back of it; not a
sentimental pretence but an idea; and an unselfish
belief in the idea—something you can set up, and
bow down before, and offer a sacrifice to. . . ."

He broke off. Flames glided in the river, small
green flames, red flames, white flames, pursuing,
overtaking, joining, crossing each other—then
separating slowly or hastily. The traffic of the
great city went on in the deepening night upon the
sleepless river. We looked on, waiting patiently—
there was nothing else to do till the end of the
flood; but it was only after a long silence, when he
said, in a hesitating voice, "I suppose you fellows
remember I did once turn fresh-water sailor for
a bit," that we knew we were fated, before the

ebb began to run, to hear about one of Marlow's inconclusive experiences.

"I don't want to bother you much with what happened to me personally," he began, showing in this remark the weakness of many tellers of tales who seem so often unaware of what their audience would like best to hear; "yet to understand the effect of it on me you ought to know how I got out there, what I saw, how I went up that river to the place where I first met the poor chap. It was the farthest point of navigation and the culminating point of my experience. It seemed somehow to throw a kind of light on everything about me—and into my thoughts. It was somber enough, too—and pitiful—not extraordinary in any way—not very clear either. No, not very clear. And yet it seemed to throw a kind of light.

"I had then, as you remember, just returned to London after a lot of Indian Ocean, Pacific, China Seas—a regular dose of the East—six years or so, and I was loafing about, hindering you fellows in your work and invading your homes, just as though I had got a heavenly mission to civilize you. It was very fine for a time, but after a bit I did get tired of resting. Then I began to look for a ship—I should think the hardest work on earth. But the ships wouldn't even look at me. And I got tired of that game, too."

"Now when I was a little chap I had a passion for maps. I would look for hours at South America, or Africa, or Australia, and lose myself in all the glories of exploration. At that time there were many blank spaces on the earth, and when I saw one that looked particularly inviting on a map (but they all look that) I would put my finger on it and say, 'When I grow up I will go there.' The North Pole was one of these places, I remember. Well, I haven't been there yet, and shall not try now. The glamour's off. Other places were scattered about the hemispheres. I have been in some of them, and . . . well, we won't talk about that. But there was one yet—the biggest, the most blank, so to speak—that I had a hankering after.

"True, by this time it was not a blank space any more. It had got filled since my boyhood with rivers and lakes and names. It had ceased to be a blank space of delightful mystery—a white patch for a boy to dream gloriously over. It had become a place of darkness. But there was in it one river especially, a mighty big river,[11] that you could see on the map, resembling an immense snake

---

[11] The Congo River

uncoiled, with its head in the sea, its body at rest curving afar over a vast country, and its tail lost in the depths of the land. And as I looked at the map of it in a shop-window, it fascinated me like a snake would a bird—a silly little bird. Then I remembered there was a big concern, a Company for trade on that river. Dash it all! I thought to myself, they can't trade without using some kind of craft on that lot of fresh water—steamboats! Why shouldn't I try to get charge of one? I went on along Fleet Street,[12] but could not shake off the idea. The snake had charmed me.

"You understand it was a Continental[13] concern, that Trading society; but I have a lot of relations living on the Continent, because it's cheap and not so nasty as it looks, they say."

"I am sorry to own I began to worry them. This was already a fresh departure for me. I was not used to get things that way, you know. I always went my own road and on my own legs where I had a mind to go. I wouldn't have believed it of myself; but, then—you see—I felt somehow I must get there by hook or by crook. So I worried them. The men said 'My dear fellow,' and did nothing.

---

[12] A major street in London
[13] Mainland Europe

Then—would you believe it?—I tried the women.
I, Charlie Marlow, set the women to work—to get
a job. Heavens! Well, you see, the notion drove
me. I had an aunt, a dear enthusiastic soul.
She wrote: 'It will be delightful. I am ready to do
anything, anything for you. It is a glorious idea.
I know the wife of a very high personage in the
Administration, and also a man who has lots of
influence with,' etc. She was determined to make
no end of fuss to get me appointed skipper of a
river steamboat, if such was my fancy."

"I got my appointment—of course; and I got it
very quick. It appears the Company had received
news that one of their captains had been killed in
a scuffle with the natives. This was my chance,
and it made me the more anxious to go. It was
only months and months afterwards, when I
made the attempt to recover what was left of the
body, that I heard the original quarrel arose from
a misunderstanding about some hens. Yes, two
black hens. Fresleven—that was the fellow's name,
a Dane—thought himself wronged somehow in
the bargain, so he went ashore and started to
hammer the chief of the village with a stick. Oh,
it didn't surprise me in the least to hear this, and
at the same time to be told that Fresleven was the
gentlest, quietest creature that ever walked on two

legs. No doubt he was; but he had been a couple
of years already out there engaged in the noble
cause, you know, and he probably felt the need
at last of asserting his self-respect in some way.
Therefore he whacked the old native[14] mercilessly,
while a big crowd of his people watched him,
thunderstruck, till some man—I was told the
chief's son—in desperation at hearing the old
chap yell, made a tentative jab with a spear at
the white man—and of course it went quite easy
between the shoulder-blades. Then the whole
population cleared into the forest, expecting all
kinds of calamities to happen, while, on the other
hand, the steamer Fresleven commanded left also
in a bad panic, in charge of the engineer, I believe.
Afterwards nobody seemed to trouble much about
Fresleven's remains, till I got out and stepped
into his shoes. I couldn't let it rest, though; but
when an opportunity offered at last to meet my
predecessor, the grass growing through his ribs
was tall enough to hide his bones. They were
all there. The supernatural being had not been
touched after he fell. And the village was deserted,
the huts gaped black, rotting, all askew within

[14] The original text here (and elsewhere) uses a derogatory racial slur.

the fallen enclosures. A calamity had come to it, sure enough. The people had vanished. Mad terror had scattered them, men, women, and children, through the bush, and they had never returned. What became of the hens I don't know either. I should think the cause of progress got them, anyhow. However, through this glorious affair I got my appointment, before I had fairly begun to hope for it.

"I flew around like mad to get ready, and before forty-eight hours I was crossing the Channel to show myself to my employers, and sign the contract. In a very few hours I arrived in a city[15] that always makes me think of a whited[16] sepulchre. Prejudice no doubt. I had no difficulty in finding the Company's offices. It was the biggest thing in the town, and everybody I met was full of it. They were going to run an over-sea empire, and make no end of coin by trade.

"A narrow and deserted street in deep shadow, high houses, innumerable windows with venetian blinds, a dead silence, grass sprouting between the stones, imposing carriage archways right and left, immense double doors standing ponderously

---

[15] Brussels, Belgium
[16] The words Christ used to describe the scribes and Pharisees in Matthew 23:27.

ajar. I slipped through one of these cracks, went up a swept and ungarnished staircase, as arid as a desert, and opened the first door I came to. Two women, one fat and the other slim, sat on straw-bottomed chairs, knitting black wool. The slim one got up and walked straight at me—still knitting with downcast eyes—and only just as I began to think of getting out of her way, as you would for a somnambulist, stood still, and looked up. Her dress was as plain as an umbrella-cover, and she turned round without a word and preceded me into a waiting-room. I gave my name, and looked about. Deal table in the middle, plain chairs all round the walls, on one end a large shining map, marked with all the colours of a rainbow. There was a vast amount of red[17]—good to see at any time, because one knows that some real work is done in there, a deuce of a lot of blue, a little green, smears of orange, and, on the East Coast, a purple patch, to show where the jolly pioneers of progress drink the jolly lager-beer. However, I wasn't going into any of these. I was going into the yellow. Dead in the centre. And the river was there—fascinating—deadly—like a snake. Ough! A door opened, a white-haired secretarial

---

[17] Red was the color that denoted territories held by Britain.

head, but wearing a compassionate expression, appeared, and a skinny forefinger beckoned me into the sanctuary. Its light was dim, and a heavy writing-desk squatted in the middle. From behind that structure came out an impression of pale plumpness in a frock-coat. The great man himself. He was five feet six, I should judge, and had his grip on the handle-end of ever so many millions. He shook hands, I fancy, murmured vaguely, was satisfied with my French. *Bon Voyage.*

"In about forty-five seconds I found myself again in the waiting-room with the compassionate secretary, who, full of desolation and sympathy, made me sign some document. I believe I undertook amongst other things not to disclose any trade secrets. Well, I am not going to.

"I began to feel slightly uneasy. You know I am not used to such ceremonies, and there was something ominous in the atmosphere. It was just as though I had been let into some conspiracy—I don't know—something not quite right; and I was glad to get out. In the outer room the two women knitted black wool feverishly. People were arriving, and the younger one was walking back and forth introducing them. The old one sat on her chair. Her flat cloth slippers were propped up on a foot-warmer, and a cat reposed on her lap. She wore

a starched white affair on her head, had a wart
on one cheek, and silver-rimmed spectacles hung
on the tip of her nose. She glanced at me above
the glasses. The swift and indifferent placidity of
that look troubled me. Two youths with foolish
and cheery countenances were being piloted over,
and she threw at them the same quick glance of
unconcerned wisdom. She seemed to know all
about them and about me, too. An eerie feeling
came over me. She seemed uncanny and fateful.
Often far away there I thought of these two,
guarding the door of Darkness, knitting black wool
as for a warm pall, one introducing, introducing
continuously to the unknown, the other scrutinizing
the cheery and foolish faces with unconcerned
old eyes. *Ave!* Old knitter of black wool. *Morituri te
salutant.*[18] Not many of those she looked at ever saw
her again—not half, by a long way.

"There was yet a visit to the doctor. 'A simple
formality,' assured me the secretary,[19] with an
air of taking an immense part in all my sorrows.

---

[18] *Hail . . . those about to die salute you*: a Latin phrase
originally offered as a salute to an emperor, here the knitter of
wool.

[19] A rare construction that is a reminder that English
is Conrad's third language—the syntax is irregular but the
grammar is correct.

Accordingly a young chap wearing his hat over
the left eyebrow, some clerk I suppose—there
must have been clerks in the business, though
the house was as still as a house in a city of
the dead—came from somewhere up-stairs,
and led me forth. He was shabby and careless,
with inkstains on the sleeves of his jacket, and
his cravat was large and billowy, under a chin
shaped like the toe of an old boot. It was a little
too early for the doctor, so I proposed a drink, and
thereupon he developed a vein of joviality. As we
sat over our vermouths he glorified the Company's
business, and by and by I expressed casually my
surprise at him not going out there. He became
very cool and collected all at once. 'I am not such
a fool as I look, quoth Plato to his disciples,' he
said sententiously, emptied his glass with great
resolution, and we rose.

"The old doctor felt my pulse, evidently
thinking of something else the while. 'Good, good
for there,' he mumbled, and then with a certain
eagerness asked me whether I would let him
measure my head. Rather surprised, I said Yes,
when he produced a thing like calipers and got
the dimensions back and front and every way,

taking notes carefully.[20] He was an unshaven little man in a threadbare coat like a gaberdine, with his feet in slippers, and I thought him a harmless fool. 'I always ask leave, in the interests of science, to measure the crania of those going out there,' he said. 'And when they come back, too?' I asked. 'Oh, I never see them,' he remarked; 'and, moreover, the changes take place inside, you know.' He smiled, as if at some quiet joke. 'So you are going out there. Famous. Interesting, too.' He gave me a searching glance, and made another note. 'Ever any madness in your family?' he asked, in a matter-of-fact tone. I felt very annoyed. 'Is that question in the interests of science, too?' 'It would be,' he said, without taking notice of my irritation, 'interesting for science to watch the mental changes of individuals, on the spot, but . . .' 'Are you an alienist?'[21] I interrupted. 'Every doctor should be—a little,' answered that original, imperturbably. 'I have a little theory which you messieurs who go out there must help me to prove. This is my share in the advantages my country shall reap from the possession of

---

[20] The doctor is practicing *phrenology*, a pseudo-science that purported to measure intellectual ability and other mental traits based on the shape and measurements of the skull.

[21] A psychiatrist

such a magnificent dependency. The mere wealth
I leave to others. Pardon my questions, but
you are the first Englishman coming under my
observation . . .' I hastened to assure him I was
not in the least typical. 'If I were,' said I, 'I wouldn't
be talking like this with you.' 'What you say is
rather profound, and probably erroneous,' he said,
with a laugh. 'Avoid irritation more than exposure
to the sun. *Adieu.* How do you English say, eh?
Good-bye. Ah! Good-bye. *Adieu.* In the tropics one
must before everything keep calm.' . . . He lifted
a warning forefinger. . . . *'Du calme, du calme.
Adieu.'*[22]

"One thing more remained to do—say good-
bye to my excellent aunt. I found her triumphant.
I had a cup of tea—the last decent cup of tea for
many days—and in a room that most soothingly
looked just as you would expect a lady's drawing-
room to look, we had a long quiet chat by the
fireside. In the course of these confidences it
became quite plain to me I had been represented
to the wife of the high dignitary, and goodness
knows to how many more people besides, as
an exceptional and gifted creature—a piece of
good fortune for the Company—a man you don't

---

[22] Keep calm, keep calm. Good bye.

get hold of every day. Good heavens! and I was going to take charge of a two-penny-half-penny river-steamboat with a penny whistle attached! It appeared, however, I was also one of the Workers,[23] with a capital—you know. Something like an emissary of light, something like a lower sort of apostle. There had been a lot of such rot let loose in print and talk just about that time, and the excellent woman, living right in the rush of all that humbug, got carried off her feet. She talked about 'weaning those ignorant millions from their horrid ways,' till, upon my word, she made me quite uncomfortable. I ventured to hint that the Company was run for profit.

"'You forget, dear Charlie, that the labourer is worthy of his hire,' she said, brightly. It's queer how out of touch with truth women are. They live in a world of their own, and there has never been anything like it, and never can be. It is too beautiful altogether, and if they were to set it up it would go to pieces before the first sunset. Some confounded fact we men have been living contentedly with ever since the day of creation would start up and knock the whole thing over.

---

[23] A Christian missionary or do-er of good works

"After this I got embraced, told to wear flannel, be sure to write often, and so on—and I left. In the street—I don't know why—a queer feeling came to me that I was an imposter. Odd thing that I, who used to clear out for any part of the world at twenty-four hours' notice, with less thought than most men give to the crossing of a street, had a moment—I won't say of hesitation, but of startled pause, before this commonplace affair. The best way I can explain it to you is by saying that, for a second or two, I felt as though, instead of going to the centre of a continent, I were about to set off for the centre of the earth.

"I left in a French steamer, and she called in every blamed port they have out there, for, as far as I could see, the sole purpose of landing soldiers and custom-house officers. I watched the coast. Watching a coast as it slips by the ship is like thinking about an enigma. There it is before you—smiling, frowning, inviting, grand, mean, insipid, or savage, and always mute with an air of whispering, 'Come and find out.' This one was almost featureless, as if still in the making, with an aspect of monotonous grimness. The edge of a colossal jungle, so dark-green as to be almost black, fringed with white surf, ran straight, like a ruled line, far, far away along a blue sea whose

glitter was blurred by a creeping mist. The sun
was fierce, the land seemed to glisten and drip
with steam. Here and there greyish-whitish specks
showed up clustered inside the white surf, with a
flag flying above them perhaps. Settlements some
centuries old, and still no bigger than pinheads
on the untouched expanse of their background.
We pounded along, stopped, landed soldiers; went
on, landed custom-house clerks to levy toll in
what looked like a God-forsaken wilderness, with
a tin shed and a flag-pole lost in it; landed more
soldiers—to take care of the custom-house clerks,
presumably. Some, I heard, got drowned in the
surf; but whether they did or not, nobody seemed
particularly to care. They were just flung out there,
and on we went. Every day the coast looked the
same, as though we had not moved; but we passed
various places—trading places—with names like
Gran' Bassam, Little Popo; names that seemed
to belong to some sordid farce acted in front of a
sinister back-cloth. The idleness of a passenger,
my isolation amongst all these men with whom I
had no point of contact, the oily and languid sea,
the uniform sombreness of the coast, seemed to
keep me away from the truth of things, within
the toils of a mournful and senseless delusion.
The voice of the surf heard now and then was a

positive pleasure, like the speech of a brother. It was something natural, that had its reason, that had a meaning. Now and then a boat from the shore gave one a momentary contact with reality. It was paddled by black fellows. You could see from afar the white of their eyeballs glistening. They shouted, sang; their bodies streamed with perspiration; they had faces like grotesque masks—these chaps; but they had bone, muscle, a wild vitality, an intense energy of movement, that was as natural and true as the surf along their coast. They wanted no excuse for being there. They were a great comfort to look at. For a time I would feel I belonged still to a world of straightforward facts; but the feeling would not last long. Something would turn up to scare it away. Once, I remember, we came upon a man-of-war anchored off the coast. There wasn't even a shed there, and she was shelling the bush. It appears the French had one of their wars going on thereabouts. Her ensign dropped limp like a rag; the muzzles of the long six-inch guns stuck out all over the low hull; the greasy, slimy swell swung her up lazily and let her down, swaying her thin masts. In the empty immensity of earth, sky, and water, there she was, incomprehensible, firing into a continent. Pop, would go one of the six-inch guns; a small flame would dart and vanish, a little white smoke would disappear, a tiny projectile would give a feeble screech—and nothing happened. Nothing could happen. There was a touch of insanity in the proceeding, a sense of lugubrious drollery in the sight; and it was not dissipated by somebody on board assuring me earnestly there was a camp of natives—he called them enemies!—hidden out of sight somewhere.

"We gave her her letters (I heard the men in that lonely ship were dying of fever at the rate of three a day) and went on. We called at some more places with farcical names, where the merry dance of death and trade goes on in a still and earthy atmosphere as of an overheated catacomb; all along the formless coast bordered by dangerous surf, as if Nature herself had tried to ward off intruders; in and out of rivers, streams of death in life, whose banks were rotting into mud, whose waters, thickened into slime, invaded the contorted mangroves, that seemed to writhe at us in the extremity of an impotent despair. Nowhere did we stop long enough to get a particularized impression, but the general sense of vague and oppressive wonder grew upon me. It was like a weary pilgrimage amongst hints for nightmares.

"It was upwards of thirty days before I saw the mouth of the big river. We anchored off the seat of the government. But my work would not begin till some two hundred miles farther on. So as soon as I could I made a start for a place thirty miles higher up.

"I had my passage on a little sea-going steamer. Her captain was a Swede, and knowing me for a seaman, invited me on the bridge. He was a young man, lean, fair, and morose, with lanky hair and a shuffling gait. As we left the miserable little wharf, he tossed his head contemptuously at the shore. 'Been living there?' he asked. I said, 'Yes.' 'Fine lot these government chaps—are they not?' he went on, speaking English with great precision and considerable bitterness. 'It is funny what some people will do for a few francs a month. I wonder what becomes of that kind when it goes upcountry?' I said to him I expected to see that soon. 'So-o-o!' he exclaimed. He shuffled athwart, keeping one eye ahead vigilantly. 'Don't be too sure,' he continued. 'The other day I took up a man who hanged himself on the road. He was a Swede, too.' 'Hanged himself! Why, in God's name?' I cried. He kept on looking out watchfully. 'Who knows? The sun too much for him, or the country perhaps.'

"At last we opened a reach. A rocky cliff appeared, mounds of turned-up earth by the shore, houses on a hill, others with iron roofs, amongst a waste of excavations, or hanging to the declivity. A continuous noise of the rapids above hovered over this scene of inhabited devastation. A lot of people, mostly black and naked, moved about like ants. A jetty projected into the river. A blinding sunlight drowned all this at times in a sudden recrudescence of glare. 'There's your Company's station,' said the Swede, pointing to three wooden barrack-like structures on the rocky slope. 'I will send your things up. Four boxes did you say? So. Farewell.'

"I came upon a boiler wallowing in the grass, then found a path leading up the hill. It turned aside for the boulders, and also for an undersized railway-truck lying there on its back with its wheels in the air. One was off. The thing looked as dead as the carcass of some animal. I came upon more pieces of decaying machinery, a stack of rusty rails. To the left a clump of trees made a shady spot, where dark things seemed to stir feebly. I blinked, the path was steep. A horn tooted to the right, and I saw the black people run. A heavy and dull detonation shook the ground, a puff of smoke came out of the cliff, and that was all. No change appeared on the face of the rock. They were building a railway. The cliff was not in the way or anything; but this objectless blasting was all the work going on.

"A slight clinking behind me made me turn my head. Six black men advanced in a file, toiling up the path. They walked erect and slow, balancing small baskets full of earth on their heads, and the clink kept time with their footsteps. Black rags were wound round their loins, and the short ends behind waggled to and fro like tails. I could see every rib, the joints of their limbs were like knots in a rope; each had an iron collar on his neck, and all were connected together with a chain whose bights swung between them, rhythmically clinking. Another report from the cliff made me think suddenly of that ship of war I had seen firing into a continent. It was the same kind of ominous voice; but these men could by no stretch of imagination be called enemies. They were called criminals, and the outraged law, like the bursting shells, had come to them, an insoluble mystery from the sea. All their meagre breasts panted together, the violently dilated nostrils quivered, the eyes stared stonily uphill. They passed me within six inches, without a glance, with that complete, deathlike indifference of unhappy savages. Behind

this raw matter one of the reclaimed, the product
of the new forces at work, strolled despondently,
carrying a rifle by its middle. He had a uniform
jacket with one button off, and seeing a white man
on the path, hoisted his weapon to his shoulder
with alacrity. This was simple prudence, white
men being so much alike at a distance that he
could not tell who I might be. He was speedily
reassured, and with a large, white, rascally grin,
and a glance at his charge, seemed to take me into
partnership in his exalted trust. After all, I also
was a part of the great cause of these high and
just proceedings.

"Instead of going up, I turned and descended
to the left. My idea was to let that chain-gang get
out of sight before I climbed the hill. You know
I am not particularly tender; I've had to strike
and to fend off. I've had to resist and to attack
sometimes—that's only one way of resisting—
without counting the exact cost, according to the
demands of such sort of life as I had blundered
into. I've seen the devil of violence, and the devil
of greed, and the devil of hot desire; but, by all the
stars! these were strong, lusty, red-eyed devils,
that swayed and drove men—men, I tell you. But
as I stood on this hillside, I foresaw that in the
blinding sunshine of that land I would become

acquainted with a flabby, pretending, weak-
eyed devil of a rapacious and pitiless folly. How
insidious he could be, too, I was only to find out
several months later and a thousand miles farther.
For a moment I stood appalled, as though by a
warning. Finally I descended the hill, obliquely,
towards the trees I had seen.

"I avoided a vast artificial hole somebody had
been digging on the slope, the purpose of which
I found it impossible to divine. It wasn't a quarry
or a sandpit, anyhow. It was just a hole. It might
have been connected with the philanthropic desire
of giving the criminals something to do. I don't
know. Then I nearly fell into a very narrow ravine,
almost no more than a scar in the hillside. I
discovered that a lot of imported drainage-pipes for
the settlement had been tumbled in there. There
wasn't one that was not broken. It was a wanton
smash-up. At last I got under the trees. My
purpose was to stroll into the shade for a moment;
but no sooner within than it seemed to me I had
stepped into the gloomy circle of some Inferno. The
rapids were near, and an uninterrupted, uniform,
headlong, rushing noise filled the mournful
stillness of the grove, where not a breath stirred,
not a leaf moved, with a mysterious sound—as

though the tearing pace of the launched earth had suddenly become audible.

"Black shapes crouched, lay, sat between the trees leaning against the trunks, clinging to the earth, half coming out, half effaced within the dim light, in all the attitudes of pain, abandonment, and despair. Another mine on the cliff went off, followed by a slight shudder of the soil under my feet. The work was going on. The work! And this was the place where some of the helpers had withdrawn to die.

"They were dying slowly—it was very clear. They were not enemies, they were not criminals, they were nothing earthly now—nothing but black shadows of disease and starvation, lying confusedly in the greenish gloom. Brought from all the recesses of the coast in all the legality of time contracts, lost in uncongenial surroundings, fed on unfamiliar food, they sickened, became inefficient, and were then allowed to crawl away and rest. These moribund shapes were free as air—and nearly as thin. I began to distinguish the gleam of the eyes under the trees. Then, glancing down, I saw a face near my hand. The black bones reclined at full length with one shoulder against the tree, and slowly the eyelids rose and the sunken eyes looked up at me, enormous and vacant, a kind of blind, white flicker in the depths of the orbs, which died out slowly. The man seemed young—almost a boy—but you know with them it's hard to tell. I found nothing else to do but to offer him one of my good Swede's ship's biscuits I had in my pocket. The fingers closed slowly on it and held—there was no other movement and no other glance. He had tied a bit of white worsted round his neck—Why? Where did he get it? Was it a badge—an ornament—a charm—a propitiatory act? Was there any idea at all connected with it? It looked startling round his black neck, this bit of white thread from beyond the seas.

"Near the same tree two more bundles of acute angles sat with their legs drawn up. One, with his chin propped on his knees, stared at nothing, in an intolerable and appalling manner: his brother phantom rested its forehead, as if overcome with a great weariness; and all about others were scattered in every pose of contorted collapse, as in some picture of a massacre or a pestilence. While I stood horror-struck, one of these creatures rose to his hands and knees, and went off on all-fours towards the river to drink. He lapped out of his hand, then sat up in the sunlight, crossing his shins in front of him, and after a time let his woolly head fall on his breastbone.

"I didn't want any more loitering in the shade, and I made haste towards the station. When near the buildings I met a white man, in such an unexpected elegance of get-up that in the first moment I took him for a sort of vision. I saw a high starched collar, white cuffs, a light alpaca jacket, snowy trousers, a clean necktie, and varnished boots. No hat. Hair parted, brushed, oiled, under a green-lined parasol held in a big white hand. He was amazing, and had a penholder behind his ear.

"I shook hands with this miracle, and I learned he was the Company's chief accountant, and that all the book-keeping was done at this station. He had come out for a moment, he said, 'to get a breath of fresh air. The expression sounded wonderfully odd, with its suggestion of sedentary desk-life. I wouldn't have mentioned the fellow to you at all, only it was from his lips that I first heard the name of the man who is so indissolubly connected with the memories of that time. Moreover, I respected the fellow. Yes; I respected his collars, his vast cuffs, his brushed hair. His appearance was certainly that of a hairdresser's dummy; but in the great demoralization of the land he kept up his appearance. That's backbone.

His starched collars and got-up shirt-fronts were achievements of character. He had been out nearly three years; and, later, I could not help asking him how he managed to sport such linen. He had just the faintest blush, and said modestly, 'I've been teaching one of the native women about the station. It was difficult. She had a distaste for the work.' Thus this man had verily accomplished something. And he was devoted to his books, which were in apple-pie order.

"Everything else in the station was in a muddle—heads, things, buildings. Strings of dusty natives with splay feet arrived and departed; a stream of manufactured goods, rubbishy cottons, beads, and brass-wire sent into the depths of darkness, and in return came a precious trickle of ivory.

"I had to wait in the station for ten days—an eternity. I lived in a hut in the yard, but to be out of the chaos I would sometimes get into the accountant's office. It was built of horizontal planks, and so badly put together that, as he bent over his high desk, he was barred from neck to heels with narrow strips of sunlight. There was no need to open the big shutter to see. It was hot there, too; big flies buzzed fiendishly, and did not sting, but stabbed. I sat generally on the floor, while, of faultless appearance (and even slightly scented), perching on a high stool, he wrote, he wrote. Sometimes he stood up for exercise. When a truckle-bed[24] with a sick man (some invalid agent from upcountry) was put in there, he exhibited a gentle annoyance. 'The groans of this sick person,' he said, 'distract my attention. And without that it is extremely difficult to guard against clerical errors in this climate.'

"One day he remarked, without lifting his head, 'In the interior you will no doubt meet Mr. Kurtz.' On my asking who Mr. Kurtz was, he said he was a first-class agent; and seeing my disappointment at this information, he added slowly, laying down his pen, 'He is a very remarkable person.' Further questions elicited from him that Mr. Kurtz was at present in charge of a trading-post, a very important one, in the true ivory-country, at 'the very bottom of there. Sends in as much ivory as all the others put together . . .' He began to write again. The sick man was too ill to groan. The flies buzzed in a great peace.

"Suddenly there was a growing murmur of voices and a great tramping of feet. A caravan had come in. A violent babble of uncouth sounds burst

_____

[24] A bed on casters or wheels, trundle bed

out on the other side of the planks. All the carriers
were speaking together, and in the midst of the
uproar the lamentable voice of the chief agent was
heard 'giving it up' tearfully for the twentieth time
that day. . . . He rose slowly. 'What a frightful row,'
he said. He crossed the room gently to look at
the sick man, and returning, said to me, 'He does
not hear.' 'What! Dead?' I asked, startled. 'No, not
yet,' he answered, with great composure. Then,
alluding with a toss of the head to the tumult
in the station-yard, 'When one has got to make
correct entries, one comes to hate those savages—
hate them to the death.' He remained thoughtful
for a moment. 'When you see Mr. Kurtz' he went
on, 'tell him from me that everything here'—he
glanced at the deck—'is very satisfactory. I don't
like to write to him—with those messengers of
ours you never know who may get hold of your
letter—at that Central Station.' He stared at me
for a moment with his mild, bulging eyes. 'Oh, he
will go far, very far,' he began again. 'He will be a
somebody in the Administration before long. They,
above—the Council in Europe, you know—mean
him to be.'

"He turned to his work. The noise outside
had ceased, and presently in going out I
stopped at the door. In the steady buzz of flies

the homeward-bound agent was lying finished and insensible; the other, bent over his books, was making correct entries of perfectly correct transactions; and fifty feet below the doorstep I could see the still tree-tops of the grove of death.

"Next day I left that station at last, with a caravan of sixty men, for a two-hundred-mile tramp.

"No use telling you much about that. Paths, paths, everywhere; a stamped-in network of paths spreading over the empty land, through the long grass, through burnt grass, through thickets, down and up chilly ravines, up and down stony hills ablaze with heat; and a solitude, a solitude, nobody, not a hut. The population had cleared out a long time ago. Well, if a lot of mysterious natives armed with all kinds of fearful weapons suddenly took to travelling on the road between Deal and Gravesend,[25] catching the yokels right and left to carry heavy loads for them, I fancy every farm and cottage thereabouts would get empty very soon. Only here the dwellings were gone, too. Still I passed through several abandoned villages. There's something pathetically childish in the ruins of grass walls. Day after day, with the stamp

---

[25] Two cities in England

and shuffle of sixty pair of bare feet behind me, each pair under a 60-lb. load. Camp, cook, sleep, strike camp, march. Now and then a carrier dead in harness, at rest in the long grass near the path, with an empty water-gourd and his long staff lying by his side. A great silence around and above. Perhaps on some quiet night the tremor of far-off drums, sinking, swelling, a tremor vast, faint; a sound weird, appealing, suggestive, and wild—and perhaps with as profound a meaning as the sound of bells in a Christian country. Once a white man in an unbuttoned uniform, camping on the path with an armed escort of lank Zanzibaris,[26] very hospitable and festive—not to say drunk. Was looking after the upkeep of the road, he declared. Can't say I saw any road or any upkeep, unless the body of a middle-aged negro, with a bullet-hole in the forehead, upon which I absolutely stumbled three miles farther on, may be considered as a permanent improvement. I had a white companion, too, not a bad chap, but rather too fleshy and with the exasperating habit of fainting on the hot hillsides, miles away from the least bit of shade and water. Annoying, you know, to hold your own coat like a parasol over a

---

[26] From a region in Tanzania

man's head while he is coming to. I couldn't help
asking him once what he meant by coming there
at all. 'To make money, of course. What do you
think?' he said, scornfully. Then he got fever, and
had to be carried in a hammock slung under a
pole. As he weighed sixteen stone[27] I had no end
of rows with the carriers. They jibbed, ran away,
sneaked off with their loads in the night—quite
a mutiny. So, one evening, I made a speech in
English with gestures, not one of which was lost
to the sixty pairs of eyes before me, and the next
morning I started the hammock off in front all
right. An hour afterwards I came upon the whole
concern wrecked in a bush—man, hammock,
groans, blankets, horrors. The heavy pole had
skinned his poor nose. He was very anxious for
me to kill somebody, but there wasn't the shadow
of a carrier near. I remembered the old doctor—'It
would be interesting for science to watch the
mental changes of individuals, on the spot.' I felt I
was becoming scientifically interesting. However,
all that is to no purpose. On the fifteenth day I
came in sight of the big river again, and hobbled
into the Central Station. It was on a back water
surrounded by scrub and forest, with a pretty

---

[27] One stone is about 14 pounds.

border of smelly mud on one side, and on the three others enclosed by a crazy fence of rushes. A neglected gap was all the gate it had, and the first glance at the place was enough to let you see the flabby devil was running that show. White men with long staves in their hands appeared languidly from amongst the buildings, strolling up to take a look at me, and then retired out of sight somewhere. One of them, a stout, excitable chap with black moustaches, informed me with great volubility and many digressions, as soon as I told him who I was, that my steamer was at the bottom of the river. I was thunderstruck. What, how, why? Oh, it was 'all right.' The 'manager himself' was there. All quite correct. 'Everybody had behaved splendidly! Splendidly!'—'You must,' he said in agitation, 'go and see the general manager at once. He is waiting!'

"I did not see the real significance of that wreck at once. I fancy I see it now, but I am not sure— not at all. Certainly the affair was too stupid— when I think of it—to be altogether natural. Still . . . But at the moment it presented itself simply as a confounded nuisance. The steamer was sunk. They had started two days before in a sudden hurry up the river with the manager on board, in charge of some volunteer skipper, and before they had been out three hours they tore the bottom out of her on stones, and she sank near the south bank. I asked myself what I was to do there, now my boat was lost. As a matter of fact, I had plenty to do in fishing my command out of the river. I had to set about it the very next day. That, and the repairs when I brought the pieces to the station, took some months.

"My first interview with the manager was curious. He did not ask me to sit down after my twenty-mile walk that morning. He was commonplace in complexion, in features, in manners, and in voice. He was of middle size and of ordinary build. His eyes, of the usual blue, were perhaps remarkably cold, and he certainly could make his glance fall on one as trenchant and heavy as an axe. But even at these times the rest of his person seemed to disclaim the intention. Otherwise there was only an indefinable, faint expression of his lips, something stealthy—a smile—not a smile—I remember it, but I can't explain. It was unconscious, this smile was, though just after he had said something it got intensified for an instant. It came at the end of his speeches like a seal applied on the words to make the meaning of the commonest phrase appear absolutely inscrutable. He was a common trader, from his youth up employed in these parts—nothing more. He was obeyed, yet he inspired neither love nor fear, nor even respect. He inspired uneasiness. That was it! Uneasiness. Not a definite mistrust—just uneasiness—nothing more. You have no idea how effective such a . . . a . . . faculty can be. He had no genius for organizing, for initiative, or for order even. That was evident in such things as the deplorable state of the station. He had no learning, and no intelligence. His position had come to him—why? Perhaps because he was never ill . . . He had served three terms of three years out there . . . Because triumphant health in the general rout of constitutions is a kind of power in itself. When he went home on leave he rioted on a large scale— pompously. Jack[28] ashore—with a difference—in externals only. This one could gather from his casual talk. He originated nothing, he could keep the routine going—that's all. But he was great. He was great by this little thing that it was impossible to tell what could control such a man. He never gave that secret away. Perhaps there was nothing within him. Such a suspicion made one pause—for

[28] Short for Jack Tar, a nickname for sailors in the Royal of Merchant Navy

out there there were no external checks. Once
when various tropical diseases had laid low almost
every 'agent' in the station, he was heard to say,
'Men who come out here should have no entrails.'
He sealed the utterance with that smile of his, as
though it had been a door opening into a darkness
he had in his keeping. You fancied you had seen
things—but the seal was on. When annoyed at
meal-times by the constant quarrels of the white
men about precedence, he ordered an immense
round table to be made, for which a special house
had to be built. This was the station's mess-
room. Where he sat was the first place—the rest
were nowhere. One felt this to be his unalterable
conviction. He was neither civil nor uncivil. He
was quiet. He allowed his 'boy'—an overfed young
native from the coast—to treat the white men,
under his very eyes, with provoking insolence.

"He began to speak as soon as he saw me. I
had been very long on the road. He could not wait.
Had to start without me. The up-river stations
had to be relieved. There had been so many
delays already that he did not know who was
dead and who was alive, and how they got on—
and so on, and so on. He paid no attention to my
explanations, and, playing with a stick of sealing-
wax, repeated several times that the situation was

'very grave, very grave.' There were rumours that
a very important station was in jeopardy, and its
chief, Mr. Kurtz, was ill. Hoped it was not true.
Mr. Kurtz was . . . I felt weary and irritable. Hang
Kurtz, I thought. I interrupted him by saying I
had heard of Mr. Kurtz on the coast. 'Ah! So they
talk of him down there,' he murmured to himself.
Then he began again, assuring me Mr. Kurtz was
the best agent he had, an exceptional man, of the
greatest importance to the Company; therefore I
could understand his anxiety. He was, he said,
'very, very uneasy.' Certainly he fidgeted on his
chair a good deal, exclaimed, 'Ah, Mr. Kurtz!' broke
the stick of sealing-wax and seemed dumfounded
by the accident. Next thing he wanted to know
'how long it would take to' . . . I interrupted him
again. Being hungry, you know, and kept on my
feet too. I was getting savage. 'How can I tell?' I
said. 'I haven't even seen the wreck yet—some
months, no doubt.' All this talk seemed to me so
futile. 'Some months,' he said. 'Well, let us say
three months before we can make a start. Yes.
That ought to do the affair.' I flung out of his
hut (he lived all alone in a clay hut with a sort of
verandah) muttering to myself my opinion of him.
He was a chattering idiot. Afterwards I took it back
when it was borne in upon me startlingly with

what extreme nicety he had estimated the time requisite for the 'affair.'

"I went to work the next day, turning, so to speak, my back on that station. In that way only it seemed to me I could keep my hold on the redeeming facts of life. Still, one must look about sometimes; and then I saw this station, these men strolling aimlessly about in the sunshine of the yard. I asked myself sometimes what it all meant. They wandered here and there with their absurd long staves in their hands, like a lot of faithless pilgrims bewitched inside a rotten fence. The word *ivory* rang in the air, was whispered, was sighed. You would think they were praying to it. A taint of imbecile rapacity blew through it all, like a whiff from some corpse. By Jove! I've never seen anything so unreal in my life. And outside, the silent wilderness surrounding this cleared speck on the earth struck me as something great and invincible, like evil or truth, waiting patiently for the passing away of this fantastic invasion.

"Oh, these months! Well, never mind. Various things happened. One evening a grass shed full of calico, cotton prints, beads, and I don't know what else, burst into a blaze so suddenly that you would have thought the earth had opened to let an avenging fire consume all that trash. I was smoking my pipe quietly by my dismantled steamer, and saw them all cutting capers in the light, with their arms lifted high, when the stout man with moustaches came tearing down to the river, a tin pail in his hand, assured me that everybody was 'behaving splendidly, splendidly,' dipped about a quart of water and tore back again. I noticed there was a hole in the bottom of his pail.

"I strolled up. There was no hurry. You see the thing had gone off like a box of matches. It had been hopeless from the very first. The flame had leaped high, driven everybody back, lighted up everything—and collapsed. The shed was already a heap of embers glowing fiercely. A native was being beaten near by. They said he had caused the fire in some way; be that as it may, he was screeching most horribly. I saw him, later on, for several days, sitting in a bit of shade looking very sick and trying to recover himself; afterwards he arose and went out—and the wilderness without a sound took him into its bosom again. As I approached the glow from the dark I found myself at the back of two men, talking. I heard the name of Kurtz pronounced, then the words, 'take advantage of this unfortunate accident.' One of the men was the manager. I wished him a good evening. 'Did you ever see anything like

it—eh? it is incredible,' he said, and walked off.
The other man remained. He was a first-class
agent, young, gentlemanly, a bit reserved, with
a forked little beard and a hooked nose. He was
stand-offish with the other agents, and they on
their side said he was the manager's spy upon
them. As to me, I had hardly ever spoken to him
before. We got into talk, and by and by we strolled
away from the hissing ruins. Then he asked me
to his room, which was in the main building of
the station. He struck a match, and I perceived
that this young aristocrat had not only a silver-
mounted dressing-case but also a whole candle all
to himself. Just at that time the manager was the
only man supposed to have any right to candles.
Native mats covered the clay walls; a collection of
spears, assegais,[29] shields, knives was hung up
in trophies. The business intrusted to this fellow
was the making of bricks—so I had been informed;
but there wasn't a fragment of a brick anywhere
in the station, and he had been there more than a
year—waiting. It seems he could not make bricks
without something, I don't know what—straw
maybe. Anyway, it could not be found there and
as it was not likely to be sent from Europe, it did

---

[29] Iron-tipped spear common to Africa

not appear clear to me what he was waiting for.
An act of special creation perhaps. However, they
were all waiting—all the sixteen or twenty pilgrims
of them—for something; and upon my word it did
not seem an uncongenial occupation, from the way
they took it, though the only thing that ever came
to them was disease—as far as I could see. They
beguiled the time by backbiting and intriguing
against each other in a foolish kind of way. There
was an air of plotting about that station, but
nothing came of it, of course. It was as unreal as
everything else—as the philanthropic pretence
of the whole concern, as their talk, as their
government, as their show of work. The only real
feeling was a desire to get appointed to a trading-
post where ivory was to be had, so that they could
earn percentages. They intrigued and slandered
and hated each other only on that account—but
as to effectually lifting a little finger—oh, no. By
heavens! there is something after all in the world
allowing one man to steal a horse while another
must not look at a halter. Steal a horse straight
out. Very well. He has done it. Perhaps he can ride.
But there is a way of looking at a halter that would
provoke the most charitable of saints into a kick.

"I had no idea why he wanted to be sociable,
but as we chatted in there it suddenly occurred

to me the fellow was trying to get at something—
in fact, pumping me. He alluded constantly to
Europe, to the people I was supposed to know
there—putting leading questions as to my
acquaintances in the sepulchral city, and so
on. His little eyes glittered like mica discs—with
curiosity—though he tried to keep up a bit of
superciliousness. At first I was astonished, but
very soon I became awfully curious to see what
he would find out from me. I couldn't possibly
imagine what I had in me to make it worth his
while. It was very pretty to see how he baffled
himself, for in truth my body was full only of chills,
and my head had nothing in it but that wretched
steamboat business. It was evident he took me
for a perfectly shameless prevaricator. At last he
got angry, and, to conceal a movement of furious
annoyance, he yawned. I rose. Then I noticed a
small sketch in oils, on a panel, representing a
woman, draped and blindfolded, carrying a lighted
torch. The background was sombre—almost black.
The movement of the woman was stately, and the
effect of the torchlight on the face was sinister.

"It arrested me, and he stood by civilly, holding
an empty half-pint champagne bottle (medical
comforts) with the candle stuck in it. To my
question he said Mr. Kurtz had painted this—in

this very station more than a year ago—while waiting for means to go to his trading post. 'Tell me, pray,' said I, 'who is this Mr. Kurtz?'

"'The chief of the Inner Station,' he answered in a short tone, looking away. 'Much obliged,' I said, laughing. 'And you are the brickmaker of the Central Station. Every one knows that.' He was silent for a while. 'He is a prodigy,' he said at last. 'He is an emissary of pity and science and progress, and devil knows what else. We want,' he began to declaim suddenly, 'for the guidance of the cause intrusted to us by Europe, so to speak, higher intelligence, wide sympathies, a singleness of purpose.' 'Who says that?' I asked. 'Lots of them,' he replied. 'Some even write that; and so *he* comes here, a special being, as you ought to know.' 'Why ought I to know?' I interrupted, really surprised. He paid no attention. 'Yes. Today he is chief of the best station, next year he will be assistant-manager, two years more and . . . but I dare-say you know what he will be in two years' time. You are of the new gang—the gang of virtue. The same people who sent him specially also recommended you. Oh, don't say no. I've my own eyes to trust.' Light dawned upon me. My dear aunt's influential acquaintances were producing an unexpected effect upon that young

man. I nearly burst into a laugh. 'Do you read
the Company's confidential correspondence?' I
asked. He hadn't a word to say. It was great fun.
'When Mr. Kurtz,' I continued, severely, 'is General
Manager, you won't have the opportunity.'

"He blew the candle out suddenly, and we went
outside. The moon had risen. Black figures strolled
about listlessly, pouring water on the glow, whence
proceeded a sound of hissing; steam ascended
in the moonlight, the beaten native groaned
somewhere. 'What a row the brute makes!' said the
indefatigable man with the moustaches, appearing
near us. 'Serve him right. Transgression—
punishment—bang! Pitiless, pitiless. That's the
only way. This will prevent all conflagrations for
the future. I was just telling the manager . . .' He
noticed my companion, and became crestfallen
all at once. 'Not in bed yet,' he said, with a kind of
servile heartiness; 'it's so natural. Ha! Danger—
agitation.' He vanished. I went on to the riverside,
and the other followed me. I heard a scathing
murmur at my ear, 'Heap of muffs—go to.' The
pilgrims could be seen in knots gesticulating,
discussing. Several had still their staves in their
hands. I verily believe they took these sticks to bed
with them. Beyond the fence the forest stood up
spectrally in the moonlight, and through that dim

stir, through the faint sounds of that lamentable courtyard, the silence of the land went home to one's very heart—its mystery, its greatness, the amazing reality of its concealed life. The hurt native moaned feebly somewhere near by, and then fetched a deep sigh that made me mend my pace away from there. I felt a hand introducing itself under my arm. 'My dear sir,' said the fellow, 'I don't want to be misunderstood, and especially by you, who will see Mr. Kurtz long before I can have that pleasure. I wouldn't like him to get a false idea of my disposition. . . .'

"I let him run on, this *papier-mache* Mephistopheles,[30] and it seemed to me that if I tried I could poke my forefinger through him, and would find nothing inside but a little loose dirt, maybe. He, don't you see, had been planning to be assistant-manager by and by under the present man, and I could see that the coming of that Kurtz had upset them both not a little. He talked precipitately, and I did not try to stop him. I had my shoulders against the wreck of my steamer, hauled up on the slope like a carcass of some big river animal. The smell of mud, of primeval mud,

---

[30] Name of a demon from German folklore and the legend of Faust

by Jove! was in my nostrils, the high stillness of primeval forest was before my eyes; there were shiny patches on the black creek. The moon had spread over everything a thin layer of silver—over the rank grass, over the mud, upon the wall of matted vegetation standing higher than the wall of a temple, over the great river I could see through a sombre gap glittering, glittering, as it flowed broadly by without a murmur. All this was great, expectant, mute, while the man jabbered about himself. I wondered whether the stillness on the face of the immensity looking at us two were meant as an appeal or as a menace. What were we who had strayed in here? Could we handle that dumb thing, or would it handle us? I felt how big, how confoundedly big, was that thing that couldn't talk, and perhaps was deaf as well. What was in there? I could see a little ivory coming out from there, and I had heard Mr. Kurtz was in there. I had heard enough about it, too—God knows! Yet somehow it didn't bring any image with it—no more than if I had been told an angel or a fiend was in there. I believed it in the same way one of you might believe there are inhabitants in the planet Mars. I knew once a Scotch sail maker who was certain, dead sure, there were people in Mars. If you asked him for some idea how they

looked and behaved, he would get shy and mutter
something about 'walking on all-fours.' If you
as much as smiled, he would—though a man of
sixty—offer to fight you. I would not have gone
so far as to fight for Kurtz, but I went for him
near enough to a lie. You know I hate, detest, and
can't bear a lie, not because I am straighter than
the rest of us, but simply because it appalls me.
There is a taint of death, a flavour of mortality
in lies—which is exactly what I hate and detest
in the world—what I want to forget. It makes me
miserable and sick, like biting something rotten
would do. Temperament, I suppose. Well, I went
near enough to it by letting the young fool there
believe anything he liked to imagine as to my
influence in Europe. I became in an instant as
much of a pretence as the rest of the bewitched
pilgrims. This simply because I had a notion it
somehow would be of help to that Kurtz whom at
the time I did not see—you understand. He was
just a word for me. I did not see the man in the
name any more than you do. Do you see him? Do
you see the story? Do you see anything? It seems
to me I am trying to tell you a dream—making a
vain attempt, because no relation of a dream can
convey the dream-sensation, that commingling of
absurdity, surprise, and bewilderment in a tremor

of struggling revolt, that notion of being captured by the incredible which is of the very essence of dreams. . . ."

He was silent for a while.

". . . No, it is impossible; it is impossible to convey the life-sensation of any given epoch of one's existence—that which makes its truth, its meaning—its subtle and penetrating essence. It is impossible. We live, as we dream—alone. . . ."

He paused again as if reflecting, then added:

"Of course in this you fellows see more than I could then. You see me, whom you know. . . ."

It had become so pitch dark that we listeners could hardly see one another. For a long time already he, sitting apart, had been no more to us than a voice. There was not a word from anybody. The others might have been asleep, but I was awake. I listened, I listened on the watch for the sentence, for the word, that would give me the clue to the faint uneasiness inspired by this narrative that seemed to shape itself without human lips in the heavy night-air of the river.

". . . Yes—I let him run on," Marlow began again, "and think what he pleased about the powers that were behind me. I did! And there was nothing behind me! There was nothing but that wretched, old, mangled steamboat I was leaning against, while he talked fluently about 'the necessity for every man to get on.' 'And when one comes out here, you conceive, it is not to gaze at the moon.' Mr. Kurtz was a 'universal genius,' but even a genius would find it easier to work with 'adequate tools—intelligent men.' He did not make bricks—why, there was a physical impossibility in the way—as I was well aware; and if he did secretarial work for the manager, it was because 'no sensible man rejects wantonly the confidence of his superiors.' Did I see it? I saw it. What more did I want? What I really wanted was rivets, by heaven! Rivets. To get on with the work—to stop the hole. Rivets I wanted. There were cases of them down at the coast—cases—piled up—burst—split! You kicked a loose rivet at every second step in that station-yard on the hillside. Rivets had rolled into the grove of death. You could fill your pockets with rivets for the trouble of stooping down— and there wasn't one rivet to be found where it was wanted. We had plates that would do, but nothing to fasten them with. And every week the messenger, a lone negro, letter-bag on shoulder and staff in hand, left our station for the coast. And several times a week a coast caravan came in with trade goods—ghastly glazed calico that made you shudder only to look at it, glass beads value about a penny a quart, confounded spotted cotton handkerchiefs. And no rivets. Three carriers could have brought all that was wanted to set that steamboat afloat.

"He was becoming confidential now, but I fancy my unresponsive attitude must have exasperated him at last, for he judged it necessary to inform me he feared neither God nor devil, let alone any mere man. I said I could see that very well, but what I wanted was a certain quantity of rivets— and rivets were what really Mr. Kurtz wanted, if he had only known it. Now letters went to the coast every week. . . . 'My dear sir,' he cried, 'I write from dictation.' I demanded rivets. There was a way—for an intelligent man. He changed his manner; became very cold, and suddenly began to talk about a hippopotamus; wondered whether sleeping on board the steamer (I stuck to my salvage night and day) I wasn't disturbed. There was an old hippo that had the bad habit of getting out on the bank and roaming at night over the station grounds. The pilgrims used to turn out in a body and empty every rifle they could lay hands on at him. Some even had sat up o' nights for him. All this energy was wasted, though. 'That animal has a charmed life,' he said; 'but you can say this only of brutes in this country. No

man—you apprehend me?—no man here bears
a charmed life.' He stood there for a moment in
the moonlight with his delicate hooked nose set a
little askew, and his mica eyes glittering without
a wink, then, with a curt "Goodnight," he strode
off. I could see he was disturbed and considerably
puzzled, which made me feel more hopeful than
I had been for days. It was a great comfort to
turn from that chap to my influential friend, the
battered, twisted, ruined, tin-pot steamboat. I
clambered on board. She rang under my feet like
an empty Huntley & Palmer biscuit-tin kicked
along a gutter; she was nothing so solid in
make, and rather less pretty in shape, but I had
expended enough hard work on her to make me
love her. No influential friend would have served
me better. She had given me a chance to come out
a bit—to find out what I could do. No, I don't like
work. I had rather laze about and think of all the
fine things that can be done. I don't like work—
no man does—but I like what is in the work—the
chance to find yourself. Your own reality—for
yourself, not for others—what no other man can
ever know. They can only see the mere show, and
never can tell what it really means.

"I was not surprised to see somebody sitting
aft, on the deck, with his legs dangling over the

mud. You see I rather chummed with the few mechanics there were in that station, whom the other pilgrims naturally despised—on account of their imperfect manners, I suppose. This was the foreman—a boilermaker by trade—a good worker. He was a lank, bony, yellow-faced man, with big intense eyes. His aspect was worried, and his head was as bald as the palm of my hand; but his hair in falling seemed to have stuck to his chin, and had prospered in the new locality, for his beard hung down to his waist. He was a widower with six young children (he had left them in charge of a sister of his to come out there), and the passion of his life was pigeon flying. He was an enthusiast and a connoisseur. He would rave about pigeons. After work hours he used sometimes to come over from his hut for a talk about his children and his pigeons; at work, when he had to crawl in the mud under the bottom of the steamboat, he would tie up that beard of his in a kind of white serviette he brought for the purpose. It had loops to go over his ears. In the evening he could be seen squatted on the bank rinsing that wrapper in the creek with great care, then spreading it solemnly on a bush to dry.

"I slapped him on the back and shouted, 'We shall have rivets!' He scrambled to his feet

exclaiming, 'No! Rivets!' as though he couldn't
believe his ears. Then in a low voice, 'You . . .
eh?' I don't know why we behaved like lunatics. I
put my finger to the side of my nose and nodded
mysteriously. 'Good for you!' he cried, snapped
his fingers above his head, lifting one foot. I tried
a jig. We capered on the iron deck. A frightful
clatter came out of that empty hulk, and the virgin
forest on the other bank of the creek sent it back
in a thundering roll upon the sleeping station. It
must have made some of the pilgrims sit up in
their hovels. A dark figure obscured the lighted
doorway of the manager's hut, vanished, then, a
second or so after, the doorway itself vanished,
too. We stopped, and the silence driven away
by the stamping of our feet flowed back again
from the recesses of the land. The great wall of
vegetation, an exuberant and entangled mass
of trunks, branches, leaves, boughs, festoons,
motionless in the moonlight, was like a rioting
invasion of soundless life, a rolling wave of plants,
piled up, crested, ready to topple over the creek,
to sweep every little man of us out of his little
existence. And it moved not. A deadened burst of
mighty splashes and snorts reached us from afar,

as though an icthyosaurus[31] had been taking a bath of glitter in the great river. 'After all,' said the boiler-maker in a reasonable tone, 'why shouldn't we get the rivets?' Why not, indeed! I did not know of any reason why we shouldn't. 'They'll come in three weeks,' I said confidently.

"But they didn't. Instead of rivets there came an invasion, an infliction, a visitation. It came in sections during the next three weeks, each section headed by a donkey carrying a white man in new clothes and tan shoes, bowing from that elevation right and left to the impressed pilgrims. A quarrelsome band of footsore sulky natives trod on the heels of the donkey; a lot of tents, camp-stools, tin boxes, white cases, brown bales would be shot down in the courtyard, and the air of mystery would deepen a little over the muddle of the station. Five such installments came, with their absurd air of disorderly flight with the loot of innumerable outfit shops and provision stores, that, one would think, they were lugging, after a raid, into the wilderness for equitable division. It was an inextricable mess of things decent in themselves but that human folly made look like the spoils of thieving.

---

[31] A large marine reptile, now extinct

"This devoted band called itself the Eldorado[32] Exploring Expedition, and I believe they were sworn to secrecy. Their talk, however, was the talk of sordid buccaneers: it was reckless without hardihood, greedy without audacity, and cruel without courage; there was not an atom of foresight or of serious intention in the whole batch of them, and they did not seem aware these things are wanted for the work of the world. To tear treasure out of the bowels of the land was their desire, with no more moral purpose at the back of it than there is in burglars breaking into a safe. Who paid the expenses of the noble enterprise I don't know; but the uncle of our manager was leader of that lot.

"In exterior he resembled a butcher in a poor neighbourhood, and his eyes had a look of sleepy cunning. He carried his fat paunch with ostentation on his short legs, and during the time his gang infested the station spoke to no one but his nephew. You could see these two roaming about all day long with their heads close together in an everlasting confab.[33]

---

[32] A legendary land of gold believed by explorers of the sixteenth and seventeenth centuries to exist in South America
[33] Short for confabulation; talk

"I had given up worrying myself about the rivets. One's capacity for that kind of folly is more limited than you would suppose. I said Hang!— and let things slide. I had plenty of time for meditation, and now and then I would give some thought to Kurtz. I wasn't very interested in him. No. Still, I was curious to see whether this man, who had come out equipped with moral ideas of some sort, would climb to the top after all and how he would set about his work when there."

PART 1
REFLECTION QUESTIONS

1. The first several paragraphs are devoted to a description of the scene that serves as the entire frame for the narrative. How does this description—and particularly the imagery—establish the overall mood and theme?

2. How are men aboard the *Nellie* character-ized? What details are given? What details are left out? Why are certain details offered but not others?

3. What are the first words spoken in the story? Whose words are they?

4. What is Marlow referring to with the word *this*?

5. Marlow says, "What saves us is efficiency." What particular place does *efficiency* have in the modern world—both Marlow's and our own? Note the presence and absence of efficiency later in the story.

6. Marlow proclaims, "The conquest of the earth, which mostly means the taking it away from those who have a different complexion or slightly flatter noses than ourselves, is not a pretty thing when you look into it too much. What redeems it is the idea only. An idea at the back of it; not a sentimental pretence but an idea; and an unselfish belief in the idea—something you can set up, and bow down before, and offer a sacrifice to. . . ." Consider this claim carefully and re-examine it after reading the entire work.

7. Marlow's use of language throughout ranges from sincere to cynical to ironic. Understanding these shifts in his tone and posture toward elements of his narrative is crucial to understanding

the story. Note these differences throughout. Find examples of when Marlow seems sincere and when he seems to be speaking with irony or sarcasm.

8. How was Marlow's view of travel and exploration as a boy developed? How might the imperialistic spirit of the late nineteenth century have helped to cultivate such desires and passions in him?

9. In recalling the maps of his youth, Marlow described the Congo without naming it. How does he describe it?

10. What person helped Marlow obtain his appointment as a steamboat skipper for the Belgian trading company?

11. What were the circumstances that provided the job opening for Marlow? What does Marlow's description of these circumstances reveal about his character, particularly when Marlow says that when he met his predecessor, "the grass growing through his ribs was tall enough to hide his bones"?

12. When Marlow undergoes a doctor's examination as part of the requirement for being employed

by the company, the doctor uses a method of examination called phrenology, which purported that character traits and intellectual abilities could be assessed by the shape of the skull. Later in Part 2, Marlow makes a comment about Kurtz's frontal bone. This nineteenth-century pseudo-science was used to prop up racist ideas that are implied throughout the story. Where are these instances and how do they reflect the racist assumptions of Marlow's society?

13. The doctor's words to Marlow remarking that the changes of "those going out there" "take place on the inside" are a moment of foreshadowing. Recall these words after reading more of the story.

14. The text devotes considerable space to Marlow's impressions of the African natives he encounters on his journey to the Congo and upon his arrival there. His description reflects the tension between his racism and his recognition of their full humanity. Note the words and phrases he uses that reveal these two conflicting attitudes. How would you describe Marlow's view of the African people?

15. Why does Marlow refer to one of the natives as "raw matter" and to one of the company men as "one of the reclaimed"? Does he use these terms sincerely or ironically?

16. How does Marlow first hear about Kurtz? What does he learn? Trace the slow development of Marlow's (and the reader's) knowledge of this mysterious man. What effect is achieved by Kurtz being revealed slowly through these accumulating bits of knowledge?

17. In response to an ill company agent's moans, the accountant tells Marlow, "'The groans of this sick person,' he said, 'distract my attention. And without that it is extremely difficult to guard against clerical errors in this climate.'" What does this statement reveal not only about the accountant but about the ethical values of the company he represents?

18. What does it say about the values of Marlow's world that the company men and the workers are identified solely by their jobs rather than their names or any other characteristic?

19. Which of the company men introduced in Part 1 seems most "hollow" or "dark" and why?

20. What does the brick maker mean when he tells Marlow that Kurtz "is an emissary of pity and science and progress"? Return to this phrase after reading the entire work and consider its significance.

21. Part 1 ends with words that point to the rest of Marlow's story and the role Kurtz has in it: "I was curious to see whether this man, who had come out equipped with moral ideas of some sort, would climb to the top after all and how he would set about his work when there." What expectations does this ending of Part 1 set up for the reader?

II

"One evening as I was lying flat on the deck of my steamboat, I heard voices approaching— and there were the nephew and the uncle strolling along the bank. I laid my head on my arm again, and had nearly lost myself in a doze, when somebody said in my ear, as it were: 'I am as harmless as a little child, but I don't like to be dictated to. Am I the manager— or am I not? I was ordered to send him there. It's incredible.' . . . I became aware that the two were standing on the shore alongside the forepart of the steamboat, just below my head. I did not move; it did not occur to me to move:

I was sleepy. 'It *is* unpleasant,' grunted the uncle. 'He has asked the Administration to be sent there,' said the other, 'with the idea of showing what he could do; and I was instructed accordingly. Look at the influence that man must have. Is it not frightful?' They both agreed it was frightful, then made several bizarre remarks: 'Make rain and fine weather—one man—the Council—by the nose'— bits of absurd sentences that got the better of my drowsiness, so that I had pretty near the whole of my wits about me when the uncle said, 'The climate may do away with this difficulty for you. Is he alone there?' 'Yes,' answered the manager; 'he sent his assistant down the river with a note to me in these terms: "Clear this poor devil out of the country, and don't bother sending more of that sort. I had rather be alone than have the kind of men you can dispose of with me." It was more than a year ago. Can you imagine such impudence!' 'Anything since then?' asked the other hoarsely. 'Ivory,' jerked out the nephew; 'lots of it— prime sort—lots—most annoying, from him.' 'And with that?' questioned the heavy rumble. 'Invoice,' was the reply fired out, so to speak. Then silence. They had been talking about Kurtz.

"I was broad awake by this time, but, lying perfectly at ease, remained still, having no

inducement to change my position. 'How did that
ivory come all this way?' growled the elder man,
who seemed very vexed. The other explained that
it had come with a fleet of canoes in charge of an
English half-caste[1] clerk Kurtz had with him; that
Kurtz had apparently intended to return himself,
the station being by that time bare of goods and
stores, but after coming three hundred miles, had
suddenly decided to go back, which he started
to do alone in a small dugout with four paddlers,
leaving the half-caste to continue down the river
with the ivory. The two fellows there seemed
astounded at anybody attempting such a thing.
They were at a loss for an adequate motive. As
to me, I seemed to see Kurtz for the first time. It
was a distinct glimpse: the dugout, four paddling
savages, and the lone white man turning his
back suddenly on the headquarters, on relief,
on thoughts of home—perhaps; setting his face
towards the depths of the wilderness, towards
his empty and desolate station. I did not know
the motive. Perhaps he was just simply a fine
fellow who stuck to his work for its own sake. His
name, you understand, had not been pronounced
once. He was 'that man.' The half-caste, who, as

---

[1] Mixed race

far as I could see, had conducted a difficult trip
with great prudence and pluck, was invariably
alluded to as 'that scoundrel.' The 'scoundrel'
had reported that the 'man' had been very ill—
had recovered imperfectly. . . . The two below me
moved away then a few paces, and strolled back
and forth at some little distance. I heard: 'Military
post—doctor—two hundred miles—quite alone
now—unavoidable delays—nine months—no
news—strange rumours.' They approached again,
just as the manager was saying, 'No one, as far as
I know, unless a species of wandering trader—a
pestilential fellow, snapping ivory from the
natives.' Who was it they were talking about now?
I gathered in snatches that this was some man
supposed to be in Kurtz's district, and of whom
the manager did not approve. 'We will not be free
from unfair competition till one of these fellows
is hanged for an example,' he said. 'Certainly,'
grunted the other; 'get him hanged! Why not?
Anything—anything can be done in this country.
That's what I say; nobody here, you understand,
here, can endanger your position. And why? You
stand the climate—you outlast them all. The
danger is in Europe; but there before I left I took
care to—' They moved off and whispered, then
their voices rose again. 'The extraordinary series of

delays is not my fault. I did my best.' The fat man
sighed. 'Very sad.' 'And the pestiferous absurdity
of his talk,' continued the other; 'he bothered me
enough when he was here. "Each station should be
like a beacon on the road towards better things, a
centre for trade of course, but also for humanizing,
improving, instructing." Conceive you—that ass!
And he wants to be manager! No, it's—' Here he
got choked by excessive indignation, and I lifted
my head the least bit. I was surprised to see how
near they were—right under me. I could have spat
upon their hats. They were looking on the ground,
absorbed in thought. The manager was switching
his leg with a slender twig: his sagacious relative
lifted his head. 'You have been well since you came
out this time?' he asked. The other gave a start.
'Who? I? Oh! Like a charm—like a charm. But the
rest—oh, my goodness! All sick. They die so quick,
too, that I haven't the time to send them out of the
country—it's incredible!' 'Hm'm. Just so,' grunted
the uncle. 'Ah! my boy, trust to this—I say, trust
to this.' I saw him extend his short flipper of an
arm for a gesture that took in the forest, the creek,
the mud, the river—seemed to beckon with a
dishonouring flourish before the sunlit face of the
land a treacherous appeal to the lurking death,
to the hidden evil, to the profound darkness of

its heart. It was so startling that I leaped to my feet and looked back at the edge of the forest, as though I had expected an answer of some sort to that black display of confidence. You know the foolish notions that come to one sometimes. The high stillness confronted these two figures with its ominous patience, waiting for the passing away of a fantastic[2] invasion.

"They swore aloud together—out of sheer fright, I believe—then pretending not to know anything of my existence, turned back to the station. The sun was low; and leaning forward side by side, they seemed to be tugging painfully uphill their two ridiculous shadows of unequal length, that trailed behind them slowly over the tall grass without bending a single blade.

"In a few days the Eldorado Expedition went into the patient wilderness, that closed upon it as the sea closes over a diver. Long afterwards the news came that all the donkeys were dead. I know nothing as to the fate of the less valuable animals. They, no doubt, like the rest of us, found what they deserved. I did not inquire. I was then rather excited at the prospect of meeting Kurtz very soon. When I say very soon I mean it comparatively. It

---

[2] In the original sense of the word: fantasy-like or unreal

was just two months from the day we left the creek
when we came to the bank below Kurtz's station.

"Going up that river was like traveling back
to the earliest beginnings of the world, when
vegetation rioted on the earth and the big trees
were kings. An empty stream, a great silence,
an impenetrable forest. The air was warm,
thick, heavy, sluggish. There was no joy in the
brilliance of sunshine. The long stretches of the
waterway ran on, deserted, into the gloom of
overshadowed distances. On silvery sand-banks
hippos and alligators sunned themselves side
by side. The broadening waters flowed through
a mob of wooded islands; you lost your way on
that river as you would in a desert, and butted
all day long against shoals, trying to find the
channel, till you thought yourself bewitched and
cut off for ever from everything you had known
once—somewhere—far away—in another existence
perhaps. There were moments when one's past
came back to one, as it will sometimes when you
have not a moment to spare for yourself; but
it came in the shape of an unrestful and noisy
dream, remembered with wonder amongst the
overwhelming realities of this strange world of
plants, and water, and silence. And this stillness
of life did not in the least resemble a peace. It was

the stillness of an implacable force brooding over
an inscrutable intention. It looked at you with
a vengeful aspect. I got used to it afterwards; I
did not see it any more; I had no time. I had to
keep guessing at the channel; I had to discern,
mostly by inspiration, the signs of hidden banks; I
watched for sunken stones; I was learning to clap
my teeth smartly before my heart flew out, when
I shaved by a fluke some infernal sly old snag
that would have ripped the life out of the tin-pot
steamboat and drowned all the pilgrims; I had
to keep a lookout for the signs of dead wood we
could cut up in the night for next day's steaming.
When you have to attend to things of that sort,
to the mere incidents of the surface, the reality—
the reality, I tell you—fades. The inner truth is
hidden—luckily, luckily. But I felt it all the same;
I felt often its mysterious stillness watching me at
my monkey tricks, just as it watches you fellows
performing on your respective tight-ropes for—
what is it? half-a-crown a tumble—"

"Try to be civil, Marlow," growled a voice, and I
knew there was at least one listener awake besides
myself.

"I beg your pardon. I forgot the heartache
which makes up the rest of the price. And indeed
what does the price matter, if the trick be well

done? You do your tricks very well. And I didn't
do badly either, since I managed not to sink that
steamboat on my first trip. It's a wonder to me
yet. Imagine a blindfolded man set to drive a van
over a bad road. I sweated and shivered over that
business considerably, I can tell you. After all,
for a seaman, to scrape the bottom of the thing
that's supposed to float all the time under his
care is the unpardonable sin. No one may know
of it, but you never forget the thump—eh? A blow
on the very heart. You remember it, you dream
of it, you wake up at night and think of it—years
after—and go hot and cold all over. I don't pretend
to say that steamboat floated all the time. More
than once she had to wade for a bit, with twenty
cannibals splashing around and pushing. We
had enlisted some of these chaps on the way for
a crew. Fine fellows—cannibals—in their place.
They were men one could work with, and I am
grateful to them. And, after all, they did not eat
each other before my face: they had brought along
a provision of hippo-meat which went rotten,
and made the mystery of the wilderness stink in
my nostrils. Phoo! I can sniff it now. I had the
manager on board and three or four pilgrims
with their staves—all complete. Sometimes we
came upon a station close by the bank, clinging

to the skirts of the unknown, and the white men rushing out of a tumble-down hovel, with great gestures of joy and surprise and welcome, seemed very strange—had the appearance of being held there captive by a spell. The word *ivory* would ring in the air for a while—and on we went again into the silence, along empty reaches, round the still bends, between the high walls of our winding way, reverberating in hollow claps the ponderous beat of the stern-wheel. Trees, trees, millions of trees, massive, immense, running up high; and at their foot, hugging the bank against the stream, crept the little begrimed steamboat, like a sluggish beetle crawling on the floor of a lofty portico. It made you feel very small, very lost, and yet it was not altogether depressing, that feeling. After all, if you were small, the grimy beetle crawled on—which was just what you wanted it to do. Where the pilgrims imagined it crawled to I don't know. To some place where they expected to get something. I bet! For me it crawled towards Kurtz—exclusively; but when the steam-pipes started leaking we crawled very slow. The reaches opened before us and closed behind, as if the forest had stepped leisurely across the water to bar the way for our return. We penetrated deeper and deeper into the heart of darkness.

It was very quiet there. At night sometimes the
roll of drums behind the curtain of trees would
run up the river and remain sustained faintly,
as if hovering in the air high over our heads, till
the first break of day. Whether it meant war,
peace, or prayer we could not tell. The dawns
were heralded by the descent of a chill stillness;
the wood-cutters slept, their fires burned low;
the snapping of a twig would make you start.
We were wanderers on a prehistoric earth, on an
earth that wore the aspect of an unknown planet.
We could have fancied ourselves the first of men
taking possession of an accursed inheritance, to
be subdued at the cost of profound anguish and
of excessive toil. But suddenly, as we struggled
round a bend, there would be a glimpse of rush
walls, of peaked grass-roofs, a burst of yells, a
whirl of black limbs, a mass of hands clapping
of feet stamping, of bodies swaying, of eyes
rolling, under the droop of heavy and motionless
foliage. The steamer toiled along slowly on the
edge of a black and incomprehensible frenzy. The
prehistoric man was cursing us, praying to us,
welcoming us—who could tell? We were cut off
from the comprehension of our surroundings;
we glided past like phantoms, wondering and
secretly appalled, as sane men would be before an

enthusiastic outbreak in a madhouse. We could
not understand because we were too far and could
not remember because we were travelling in the
night of first ages, of those ages that are gone,
leaving hardly a sign—and no memories.

"The earth seemed unearthly. We are
accustomed to look upon the shackled form
of a conquered monster, but there—there you
could look at a thing monstrous and free. It was
unearthly, and the men were—No, they were not
inhuman. Well, you know, that was the worst of
it—this suspicion of their not being inhuman.
It would come slowly to one. They howled and
leaped, and spun, and made horrid faces; but
what thrilled you was just the thought of their
humanity—like yours—the thought of your remote
kinship with this wild and passionate uproar.
Ugly. Yes, it was ugly enough; but if you were man
enough you would admit to yourself that there was
in you just the faintest trace of a response to the
terrible frankness of that noise, a dim suspicion
of there being a meaning in it which you—you
so remote from the night of first ages—could
comprehend. And why not? The mind of man is
capable of anything—because everything is in it,
all the past as well as all the future. What was
there after all? Joy, fear, sorrow, devotion, valour,

rage—who can tell?—but truth—truth stripped of its cloak of time. Let the fool gape and shudder—the man knows, and can look on without a wink. But he must at least be as much of a man as these on the shore. He must meet that truth with his own true stuff—with his own inborn strength. Principles. Principles wouldn't do. Acquisitions, clothes, pretty rags—rags that would fly off at the first good shake. No; you want a deliberate belief. An appeal to me in this fiendish row—is there? Very well; I hear; I admit, but I have a voice, too, and for good or evil mine is the speech that cannot be silenced. Of course, a fool, what with sheer fright and fine sentiments, is always safe. Who's that grunting? You wonder I didn't go ashore for a howl and a dance? Well, no—I didn't. Fine sentiments, you say? Fine sentiments, be hanged! I had no time. I had to mess about with white lead and strips of woolen blanket helping to put bandages on those leaky steam-pipes—I tell you. I had to watch the steering, and circumvent those snags, and get the tin-pot along by hook or by crook. There was surface-truth enough in these things to save a wiser man. And between whiles I had to look after the savage who was fireman. He was an improved specimen; he could fire up a vertical boiler. He was there below me, and,

upon my word, to look at him was as edifying as
seeing a dog in a parody of breeches and a feather
hat, walking on his hind-legs. A few months of
training had done for that really fine chap. He
squinted at the steam-gauge and at the water-
gauge with an evident effort of intrepidity—and he
had filed teeth, too, the poor devil, and the wool
of his pate shaved into queer patterns, and three
ornamental scars on each of his cheeks. He ought
to have been clapping his hands and stamping
his feet on the bank, instead of which he was
hard at work, a thrall to strange witchcraft, full of
improving knowledge. He was useful because he
had been instructed; and what he knew was this—
that should the water in that transparent thing
disappear, the evil spirit inside the boiler would
get angry through the greatness of his thirst, and
take a terrible vengeance. So he sweated and
fired up and watched the glass fearfully (with an
impromptu charm, made of rags, tied to his arm,
and a piece of polished bone, as big as a watch,
stuck flatways through his lower lip), while the
wooded banks slipped past us slowly, the short
noise was left behind, the interminable miles of
silence—and we crept on, towards Kurtz. But the
snags were thick, the water was treacherous and
shallow, the boiler seemed indeed to have a sulky

devil in it, and thus neither that fireman nor I had any time to peer into our creepy thoughts.

"Some fifty miles below the Inner Station we came upon a hut of reeds, an inclined and melancholy pole, with the unrecognizable tatters of what had been a flag of some sort flying from it, and a neatly stacked wood-pile. This was unexpected. We came to the bank, and on the stack of firewood found a flat piece of board with some faded pencil-writing on it. When deciphered it said: 'Wood for you. Hurry up. Approach cautiously.' There was a signature, but it was illegible—not Kurtz—a much longer word. 'Hurry up.' Where? Up the river? 'Approach cautiously.' We had not done so. But the warning could not have been meant for the place where it could be only found after approach. Something was wrong above. But what—and how much? That was the question. We commented adversely upon the imbecility of that telegraphic style. The bush around said nothing, and would not let us look very far, either. A torn curtain of red twill hung in the doorway of the hut, and flapped sadly in our faces. The dwelling was dismantled; but we could see a white man had lived there not very long ago. There remained a rude table—a plank on two posts; a heap of rubbish reposed in a

dark corner, and by the door I picked up a book.
It had lost its covers, and the pages had been
thumbed into a state of extremely dirty softness;
but the back had been lovingly stitched afresh
with white cotton thread, which looked clean
yet. It was an extraordinary find. Its title was,
An Inquiry into some Points of Seamanship, by a
man Towser, Towson—some such name—Master
in his Majesty's Navy. The matter looked dreary
reading enough, with illustrative diagrams and
repulsive tables of figures, and the copy was sixty
years old. I handled this amazing antiquity with
the greatest possible tenderness, lest it should
dissolve in my hands. Within, Towson or Towser
was inquiring earnestly into the breaking strain of
ships' chains and tackle, and other such matters.
Not a very enthralling book; but at the first glance
you could see there a singleness of intention, an
honest concern for the right way of going to work,
which made these humble pages, thought out so
many years ago, luminous with another than a
professional light. The simple old sailor, with his
talk of chains and purchases, made me forget the
jungle and the pilgrims in a delicious sensation of
having come upon something unmistakably real.
Such a book being there was wonderful enough;
but still more astounding were the notes pencilled

in the margin, and plainly referring to the text. I couldn't believe my eyes! They were in cipher! Yes, it looked like cipher. Fancy a man lugging with him a book of that description into this nowhere and studying it—and making notes—in cipher[3] at that! It was an extravagant mystery.

"I had been dimly aware for some time of a worrying noise, and when I lifted my eyes I saw the wood-pile was gone, and the manager, aided by all the pilgrims, was shouting at me from the riverside. I slipped the book into my pocket. I assure you to leave off reading was like tearing myself away from the shelter of an old and solid friendship.

"I started the lame engine ahead. 'It must be this miserable trader—this intruder,' exclaimed the manager, looking back malevolently at the place we had left. 'He must be English,' I said. 'It will not save him from getting into trouble if he is not careful,' muttered the manager darkly. I observed with assumed innocence that no man was safe from trouble in this world.

"The current was more rapid now, the steamer seemed at her last gasp, the stern-wheel flopped languidly, and I caught myself listening on tiptoe

---

[3] Code

for the next beat of the boat, for in sober truth
I expected the wretched thing to give up every
moment. It was like watching the last flickers of
a life. But still we crawled. Sometimes I would
pick out a tree a little way ahead to measure our
progress towards Kurtz by, but I lost it invariably
before we got abreast. To keep the eyes so long
on one thing was too much for human patience.
The manager displayed a beautiful resignation. I
fretted and fumed and took to arguing with myself
whether or no I would talk openly with Kurtz; but
before I could come to any conclusion it occurred
to me that my speech or my silence, indeed any
action of mine, would be a mere futility. What did
it matter what any one knew or ignored? What did
it matter who was manager? One gets sometimes
such a flash of insight. The essentials of this affair
lay deep under the surface, beyond my reach, and
beyond my power of meddling.

"Towards the evening of the second day we
judged ourselves about eight miles from Kurtz's
station. I wanted to push on; but the manager
looked grave, and told me the navigation up there
was so dangerous that it would be advisable, the
sun being very low already, to wait where we were
till next morning. Moreover, he pointed out that
if the warning to approach cautiously were to be

followed, we must approach in daylight—not at dusk or in the dark. This was sensible enough. Eight miles meant nearly three hours' steaming for us, and I could also see suspicious ripples at the upper end of the reach. Nevertheless, I was annoyed beyond expression at the delay, and most unreasonably, too, since one night more could not matter much after so many months. As we had plenty of wood, and caution was the word, I brought up in the middle of the stream. The reach was narrow, straight, with high sides like a railway cutting. The dusk came gliding into it long before the sun had set. The current ran smooth and swift, but a dumb immobility sat on the banks. The living trees, lashed together by the creepers and every living bush of the undergrowth, might have been changed into stone, even to the slenderest twig, to the lightest leaf. It was not sleep—it seemed unnatural, like a state of trance. Not the faintest sound of any kind could be heard. You looked on amazed, and began to suspect yourself of being deaf—then the night came suddenly, and struck you blind as well. About three in the morning some large fish leaped, and the loud splash made me jump as though a gun had been fired. When the sun rose there was a white fog, very warm and clammy, and

more blinding than the night. It did not shift or
drive; it was just there, standing all round you like
something solid. At eight or nine, perhaps, it lifted
as a shutter lifts. We had a glimpse of the towering
multitude of trees, of the immense matted jungle,
with the blazing little ball of the sun hanging
over it—all perfectly still—and then the white
shutter came down again, smoothly, as if sliding
in greased grooves. I ordered the chain, which we
had begun to heave in, to be paid out again. Before
it stopped running with a muffled rattle, a cry,
a very loud cry, as of infinite desolation, soared
slowly in the opaque air. It ceased. A complaining
clamour, modulated in savage discords, filled our
ears. The sheer unexpectedness of it made my
hair stir under my cap. I don't know how it struck
the others: to me it seemed as though the mist
itself had screamed, so suddenly, and apparently
from all sides at once, did this tumultuous and
mournful uproar arise. It culminated in a hurried
outbreak of almost intolerably excessive shrieking,
which stopped short, leaving us stiffened in a
variety of silly attitudes, and obstinately listening
to the nearly as appalling and excessive silence.
'Good God! What is the meaning—' stammered
at my elbow one of the pilgrims—a little fat man,
with sandy hair and red whiskers, who wore

sidespring boots, and pink pajamas tucked into his socks. Two others remained open-mouthed a whole minute, then dashed into the little cabin, to rush out incontinently and stand darting scared glances, with Winchesters at 'ready' in their hands. What we could see was just the steamer we were on, her outlines blurred as though she had been on the point of dissolving, and a misty strip of water, perhaps two feet broad, around her—and that was all. The rest of the world was nowhere, as far as our eyes and ears were concerned. Just nowhere. Gone, disappeared; swept off without leaving a whisper or a shadow behind.

"I went forward, and ordered the chain to be hauled in short, so as to be ready to trip the anchor and move the steamboat at once if necessary. 'Will they attack?' whispered an awed voice. 'We will be all butchered in this fog,' murmured another. The faces twitched with the strain, the hands trembled slightly, the eyes forgot to wink. It was very curious to see the contrast of expressions of the white men and of the black fellows of our crew, who were as much strangers to that part of the river as we, though their homes were only eight hundred miles away. The whites, of course greatly discomposed, had besides a curious look of being painfully shocked

by such an outrageous row. The others had an
alert, naturally interested expression; but their
faces were essentially quiet, even those of the one
or two who grinned as they hauled at the chain.
Several exchanged short, grunting phrases, which
seemed to settle the matter to their satisfaction.
Their headman, a young, broad-chested black,
severely draped in dark-blue fringed cloths, with
fierce nostrils and his hair all done up artfully in
oily ringlets, stood near me. 'Aha!' I said, just for
good fellowship's sake. 'Catch 'im,' he snapped,
with a bloodshot widening of his eyes and a flash
of sharp teeth—'catch 'im. Give 'im to us.' 'To
you, eh?' I asked; 'what would you do with them?'
'Eat 'im!' he said curtly, and, leaning his elbow
on the rail, looked out into the fog in a dignified
and profoundly pensive attitude. I would no
doubt have been properly horrified, had it not
occurred to me that he and his chaps must be
very hungry: that they must have been growing
increasingly hungry for at least this month past.
They had been engaged for six months (I don't
think a single one of them had any clear idea of
time, as we at the end of countless ages have.
They still belonged to the beginnings of time—
had no inherited experience to teach them as it
were), and of course, as long as there was a piece

of paper written over in accordance with some
farcical law or other made down the river, it didn't
enter anybody's head to trouble how they would
live. Certainly they had brought with them some
rotten hippo-meat, which couldn't have lasted
very long, anyway, even if the pilgrims hadn't,
in the midst of a shocking hullabaloo, thrown a
considerable quantity of it overboard. It looked
like a high-handed proceeding; but it was really a
case of legitimate self-defence. You can't breathe
dead hippo waking, sleeping, and eating, and
at the same time keep your precarious grip on
existence. Besides that, they had given them every
week three pieces of brass wire, each about nine
inches long; and the theory was they were to buy
their provisions with that currency in riverside
villages. You can see how *that* worked. There were
either no villages, or the people were hostile, or
the director, who like the rest of us fed out of tins,
with an occasional old he-goat thrown in, didn't
want to stop the steamer for some more or less
recondite reason. So, unless they swallowed the
wire itself, or made loops of it to snare the fishes
with, I don't see what good their extravagant
salary could be to them. I must say it was paid
with a regularity worthy of a large and honourable
trading company. For the rest, the only thing to

eat—though it didn't look eatable in the least—I
saw in their possession was a few lumps of some
stuff like half-cooked dough, of a dirty lavender
colour, they kept wrapped in leaves, and now and
then swallowed a piece of, but so small that it
seemed done more for the looks of the thing than
for any serious purpose of sustenance. Why in
the name of all the gnawing devils of hunger they
didn't go for us—they were thirty to five—and have
a good tuck-in for once, amazes me now when I
think of it. They were big powerful men, with not
much capacity to weigh the consequences, with
courage, with strength, even yet, though their
skins were no longer glossy and their muscles no
longer hard. And I saw that something restraining,
one of those human secrets that baffle probability,
had come into play there. I looked at them with
a swift quickening of interest—not because it
occurred to me I might be eaten by them before
very long, though I own to you that just then
I perceived—in a new light, as it were—how
unwholesome the pilgrims looked, and I hoped,
yes, I positively hoped, that my aspect was not
so—what shall I say?—so—unappetizing: a touch
of fantastic vanity which fitted well with the
dream-sensation that pervaded all my days at that
time. Perhaps I had a little fever, too. One can't

live with one's finger everlastingly on one's pulse. I had often 'a little fever,' or a little touch of other things—the playful paw-strokes of the wilderness, the preliminary trifling before the more serious onslaught which came in due course. Yes; I looked at them as you would on any human being, with a curiosity of their impulses, motives, capacities, weaknesses, when brought to the test of an inexorable physical necessity. Restraint! What possible restraint? Was it superstition, disgust, patience, fear—or some kind of primitive honour? No fear can stand up to hunger, no patience can wear it out, disgust simply does not exist where hunger is; and as to superstition, beliefs, and what you may call principles, they are less than chaff in a breeze. Don't you know the devilry of lingering starvation, its exasperating torment, its black thoughts, its sombre and brooding ferocity? Well, I do. It takes a man all his inborn strength to fight hunger properly. It's really easier to face bereavement, dishonour, and the perdition of one's soul—than this kind of prolonged hunger. Sad, but true. And these chaps, too, had no earthly reason for any kind of scruple. Restraint! I would just as soon have expected restraint from a hyena prowling amongst the corpses of a battlefield. But there was the fact facing me—the fact dazzling,

to be seen, like the foam on the depths of the
sea, like a ripple on an unfathomable enigma, a
mystery greater—when I thought of it—than the
curious, inexplicable note of desperate grief in this
savage clamour that had swept by us on the river-
bank, behind the blind whiteness of the fog.

"Two pilgrims were quarrelling in hurried
whispers as to which bank. 'Left.' 'no, no; how can
you? Right, right, of course.' 'It is very serious,'
said the manager's voice behind me; 'I would be
desolated if anything should happen to Mr. Kurtz
before we came up.' I looked at him, and had
not the slightest doubt he was sincere. He was
just the kind of man who would wish to preserve
appearances. That was his restraint. But when he
muttered something about going on at once, I did
not even take the trouble to answer him. I knew,
and he knew, that it was impossible. Were we to let
go our hold of the bottom, we would be absolutely
in the air—in space. We wouldn't be able to tell
where we were going to—whether up or down
stream, or across—till we fetched against one bank
or the other—and then we wouldn't know at first
which it was. Of course I made no move. I had
no mind for a smash-up. You couldn't imagine a
more deadly place for a shipwreck. Whether we
drowned at once or not, we were sure to perish

speedily in one way or another. 'I authorize you to take all the risks,' he said, after a short silence. 'I refuse to take any,' I said shortly; which was just the answer he expected, though its tone might have surprised him. 'Well, I must defer to your judgment. You are captain,' he said with marked civility. I turned my shoulder to him in sign of my appreciation, and looked into the fog. How long would it last? It was the most hopeless lookout. The approach to this Kurtz grubbing for ivory in the wretched bush was beset by as many dangers as though he had been an enchanted princess sleeping in a fabulous castle. 'Will they attack, do you think?' asked the manager, in a confidential tone.

"I did not think they would attack, for several obvious reasons. The thick fog was one. If they left the bank in their canoes they would get lost in it, as we would be if we attempted to move. Still, I had also judged the jungle of both banks quite impenetrable—and yet eyes were in it, eyes that had seen us. The riverside bushes were certainly very thick; but the undergrowth behind was evidently penetrable. However, during the short lift I had seen no canoes anywhere in the reach—certainly not abreast of the steamer. But what made the idea of attack inconceivable to me was the nature of the noise—of the cries we had heard. They had not the fierce character boding immediate hostile intention. Unexpected, wild, and violent as they had been, they had given me an irresistible impression of sorrow. The glimpse of the steamboat had for some reason filled those savages with unrestrained grief. The danger, if any, I expounded, was from our proximity to a great human passion let loose. Even extreme grief may ultimately vent itself in violence—but more generally takes the form of apathy. . . .

"You should have seen the pilgrims stare! They had no heart to grin, or even to revile me: but I believe they thought me gone mad—with fright, maybe. I delivered a regular lecture. My dear boys, it was no good bothering. Keep a lookout? Well, you may guess I watched the fog for the signs of lifting as a cat watches a mouse; but for anything else our eyes were of no more use to us than if we had been buried miles deep in a heap of cotton-wool. It felt like it, too—choking, warm, stifling. Besides, all I said, though it sounded extravagant, was absolutely true to fact. What we afterwards alluded to as an attack was really an attempt at repulse. The action was very far from being aggressive—it was not even defensive, in the usual sense: it was undertaken under the stress of desperation, and in its essence was purely protective.

"It developed itself, I should say, two hours after the fog lifted, and its commencement was at a spot, roughly speaking, about a mile and a half below Kurtz's station. We had just floundered and flopped round a bend, when I saw an islet, a mere grassy hummock of bright green, in the middle of the stream. It was the only thing of the kind; but as we opened the reach more, I perceived it was the head of a long sand-bank, or rather of a chain of shallow patches stretching down the middle of the river. They were discoloured, just awash, and the whole lot was seen just under the water, exactly as a man's backbone is seen running down the middle of his back under the skin. Now, as far as I did see, I could go to the right or to the left of this. I didn't know either channel, of course. The banks looked pretty well alike, the depth appeared the same; but as I had been informed the station was on the west side, I naturally headed for the western passage.

"No sooner had we fairly entered it than I became aware it was much narrower than I had supposed. To the left of us there was the long uninterrupted shoal, and to the right a high, steep bank heavily overgrown with bushes. Above the bush the trees stood in serried ranks. The twigs overhung the current thickly, and from distance to distance a large limb of some tree projected rigidly over the stream. It was then well on in the afternoon, the face of the forest was gloomy, and a broad strip of shadow had already fallen on the water. In this shadow we steamed up—very slowly, as you may imagine. I sheered her well inshore—the water being deepest near the bank, as the sounding-pole informed me.

"One of my hungry and forbearing friends was sounding in the bows just below me. This steamboat was exactly like a decked scow.[4] On the deck, there were two little teakwood houses, with doors and windows. The boiler was in the fore-end, and the machinery right astern. Over the whole there was a light roof, supported on stanchions. The funnel projected through that roof, and in front of the funnel a small cabin built of light planks served for a pilot-house. It contained a couch, two camp-stools, a loaded Martini-Henry[5] leaning in one corner, a tiny table, and the steering-wheel. It had a wide door in front and a broad shutter at each side. All these were

---

[4] A flat-bottomed sailboat
[5] A single-shot British military rifle

always thrown open, of course. I spent my days
perched up there on the extreme fore-end of that
roof, before the door. At night I slept, or tried to,
on the couch. An athletic black belonging to some
coast tribe and educated by my poor predecessor,
was the helmsman. He sported a pair of brass
earrings, wore a blue cloth wrapper from the waist
to the ankles, and thought all the world of himself.
He was the most unstable kind of fool I had ever
seen. He steered with no end of a swagger while
you were by; but if he lost sight of you, he became
instantly the prey of an abject funk, and would let
that cripple of a steamboat get the upper hand of
him in a minute.

"I was looking down at the sounding-pole, and
feeling much annoyed to see at each try a little
more of it stick out of that river, when I saw my
poleman give up on the business suddenly, and
stretch himself flat on the deck, without even
taking the trouble to haul his pole in. He kept
hold on it though, and it trailed in the water. At
the same time the fireman, whom I could also see
below me, sat down abruptly before his furnace
and ducked his head. I was amazed. Then I had to
look at the river mighty quick, because there was a
snag in the fairway. Sticks, little sticks, were flying
about—thick: they were whizzing before my nose,

dropping below me, striking behind me against my pilot-house. All this time the river, the shore, the woods, were very quiet—perfectly quiet. I could only hear the heavy splashing thump of the stern-wheel and the patter of these things. We cleared the snag clumsily. Arrows, by Jove! We were being shot at! I stepped in quickly to close the shutter on the landside. That fool-helmsman, his hands on the spokes, was lifting his knees high, stamping his feet, champing his mouth, like a reined-in horse. Confound him! And we were staggering within ten feet of the bank. I had to lean right out to swing the heavy shutter, and I saw a face amongst the leaves on the level with my own, looking at me very fierce and steady; and then suddenly, as though a veil had been removed from my eyes, I made out, deep in the tangled gloom, naked breasts, arms, legs, glaring eyes—the bush was swarming with human limbs in movement, glistening of bronze colour. The twigs shook, swayed, and rustled, the arrows flew out of them, and then the shutter came to. 'Steer her straight,' I said to the helmsman. He held his head rigid, face forward; but his eyes rolled, he kept on lifting and setting down his feet gently, his mouth foamed a little. 'Keep quiet!' I said in a fury. I might just as well have ordered a tree not to sway in the wind.

I darted out. Below me there was a great scuffle
of feet on the iron deck; confused exclamations;
a voice screamed, 'Can you turn back?' I caught
sight of a V-shaped ripple on the water ahead.
What? Another snag! A fusillade burst out under
my feet. The pilgrims had opened with their
Winchesters, and were simply squirting lead
into that bush. A deuce of a lot of smoke came
up and drove slowly forward. I swore at it. Now I
couldn't see the ripple or the snag either. I stood
in the doorway, peering, and the arrows came in
swarms. They might have been poisoned, but they
looked as though they wouldn't kill a cat. The
bush began to howl. Our wood-cutters raised a
warlike whoop; the report of a rifle just at my back
deafened me. I glanced over my shoulder, and the
pilot-house was yet full of noise and smoke when
I made a dash at the wheel. The fool-native had
dropped everything, to throw the shutter open
and let off that Martini-Henry. He stood before
the wide opening, glaring, and I yelled at him to
come back, while I straightened the sudden twist
out of that steamboat. There was no room to turn
even if I had wanted to, the snag was somewhere
very near ahead in that confounded smoke, there
was no time to lose, so I just crowded her into the

bank—right into the bank, where I knew the water was deep.

"We tore slowly along the overhanging bushes in a whirl of broken twigs and flying leaves. The fusillade[6] below stopped short, as I had foreseen it would when the squirts[7] got empty. I threw my head back to a glinting whizz that traversed the pilot-house, in at one shutter-hole and out at the other. Looking past that mad helmsman, who was shaking the empty rifle and yelling at the shore, I saw vague forms of men running bent double, leaping, gliding, distinct, incomplete, evanescent. Something big appeared in the air before the shutter, the rifle went overboard, and the man stepped back swiftly, looked at me over his shoulder in an extraordinary, profound, familiar manner, and fell upon my feet. The side of his head hit the wheel twice, and the end of what appeared a long cane clattered round and knocked over a little camp-stool. It looked as though after wrenching that thing from somebody ashore he had lost his balance in the effort. The thin smoke had blown away, we were clear of the snag, and looking ahead I could see that in

---

[6] Rapid succession of shots (in this case from arrows)
[7] The firearms

another hundred yards or so I would be free to
sheer off, away from the bank; but my feet felt so
very warm and wet that I had to look down. The
man had rolled on his back and stared straight up
at me; both his hands clutched that cane. It was
the shaft of a spear that, either thrown or lunged
through the opening, had caught him in the side,
just below the ribs; the blade had gone in out of
sight, after making a frightful gash; my shoes
were full; a pool of blood lay very still, gleaming
dark-red under the wheel; his eyes shone with an
amazing lustre. The fusillade burst out again. He
looked at me anxiously, gripping the spear like
something precious, with an air of being afraid I
would try to take it away from him. I had to make
an effort to free my eyes from his gaze and attend
to the steering. With one hand I felt above my
head for the line of the steam whistle, and jerked
out screech after screech hurriedly. The tumult of
angry and warlike yells was checked instantly, and
then from the depths of the woods went out such
a tremulous and prolonged wail of mournful fear
and utter despair as may be imagined to follow
the flight of the last hope from the earth. There
was a great commotion in the bush; the shower
of arrows stopped, a few dropping shots rang out
sharply—then silence, in which the languid beat

of the stern-wheel came plainly to my ears. I put
the helm hard a-starboard at the moment when
the pilgrim in pink pajamas, very hot and agitated,
appeared in the doorway. 'The manager sends
me—' he began in an official tone, and stopped
short. 'Good God!' he said, glaring at the wounded
man.

"We two whites stood over him, and his
lustrous and inquiring glance enveloped us both.
I declare it looked as though he would presently
put to us some questions in an understandable
language; but he died without uttering a sound,
without moving a limb, without twitching a
muscle. Only in the very last moment, as though
in response to some sign we could not see, to some
whisper we could not hear, he frowned heavily,
and that frown gave to his black death-mask an
inconceivably sombre, brooding, and menacing
expression. The lustre of inquiring glance faded
swiftly into vacant glassiness. 'Can you steer?' I
asked the agent eagerly. He looked very dubious;
but I made a grab at his arm, and he understood
at once I meant him to steer whether or no. To tell
you the truth, I was morbidly anxious to change
my shoes and socks. 'He is dead,' murmured the
fellow, immensely impressed. 'No doubt about it,'
said I, tugging like mad at the shoe-laces. 'And by

the way, I suppose Mr. Kurtz is dead as well by this time.'

"For the moment that was the dominant thought. There was a sense of extreme disappointment, as though I had found out I had been striving after something altogether without a substance. I couldn't have been more disgusted if I had travelled all this way for the sole purpose of talking with Mr. Kurtz. Talking with . . . I flung one shoe overboard, and became aware that that was exactly what I had been looking forward to—a talk with Kurtz. I made the strange discovery that I had never imagined him as doing, you know, but as discoursing. I didn't say to myself, 'Now I will never see him,' or 'Now I will never shake him by the hand,' but, 'Now I will never hear him.' The man presented himself as a voice. Not of course that I did not connect him with some sort of action. Hadn't I been told in all the tones of jealousy and admiration that he had collected, bartered, swindled, or stolen more ivory than all the other agents together? That was not the point. The point was in his being a gifted creature, and that of all his gifts the one that stood out preeminently, that carried with it a sense of real presence, was his ability to talk, his words—the gift of expression, the bewildering, the illuminating, the most exalted and the most contemptible, the pulsating stream of light, or the deceitful flow from the heart of an impenetrable darkness.

"The other shoe went flying unto the devil-god of that river. I thought, 'By Jove! it's all over. We are too late; he has vanished—the gift has vanished, by means of some spear, arrow, or club. I will never hear that chap speak after all'— and my sorrow had a startling extravagance of emotion, even such as I had noticed in the howling sorrow of these savages in the bush. I couldn't have felt more of lonely desolation somehow, had I been robbed of a belief or had missed my destiny in life. . . . Why do you sigh in this beastly way, somebody? Absurd? Well, absurd. Good Lord! mustn't a man ever—Here, give me some tobacco.". . .

There was a pause of profound stillness, then a match flared, and Marlow's lean face appeared, worn, hollow, with downward folds and dropped eyelids, with an aspect of concentrated attention; and as he took vigorous draws at his pipe, it seemed to retreat and advance out of the night in the regular flicker of tiny flame. The match went out.

"Absurd!" he cried. "This is the worst of trying to tell. . . . Here you all are, each moored with two good addresses, like a hulk with two anchors, a butcher round one corner, a policeman round another, excellent appetites, and temperature normal—you hear—normal from year's end to year's end. And you say, Absurd! Absurd be— exploded! Absurd! My dear boys, what can you expect from a man who out of sheer nervousness had just flung overboard a pair of new shoes! Now I think of it, it is amazing I did not shed tears. I am, upon the whole, proud of my fortitude. I was cut to the quick at the idea of having lost the inestimable privilege of listening to the gifted Kurtz. Of course I was wrong. The privilege was waiting for me. Oh, yes, I heard more than enough. And I was right, too. A voice. He was very little more than a voice. And I heard—him— it—this voice—other voices—all of them were so little more than voices—and the memory of that time itself lingers around me, impalpable, like a dying vibration of one immense jabber, silly, atrocious, sordid, savage, or simply mean, without any kind of sense. Voices, voices—even the girl herself—now—"

He was silent for a long time.

"I laid the ghost of his gifts at last with a lie," he began, suddenly. "Girl! What? Did I mention a girl? Oh, she is out of it—completely. They—the women,

I mean—are out of it—should be out of it. We must help them to stay in that beautiful world of their own, lest ours gets worse. Oh, she had to be out of it. You should have heard the disinterred body of Mr. Kurtz saying, 'My Intended.' You would have perceived directly then how completely she was out of it. And the lofty frontal bone of Mr. Kurtz! They say the hair goes on growing sometimes, but this—ah—specimen, was impressively bald. The wilderness had patted him on the head, and, behold, it was like a ball—an ivory ball; it had caressed him, and—lo!—he had withered; it had taken him, loved him, embraced him, got into his veins, consumed his flesh, and sealed his soul to its own by the inconceivable ceremonies of some devilish initiation. He was its spoiled and pampered favourite. Ivory? I should think so. Heaps of it, stacks of it. The old mud shanty was bursting with it. You would think there was not a single tusk left either above or below the ground in the whole country. 'Mostly fossil,' the manager had remarked, disparagingly. It was no more fossil than I am; but they call it fossil when it is dug up. It appears these natives do bury the tusks sometimes—but evidently they couldn't bury this parcel deep enough to save the gifted Mr. Kurtz from his fate. We filled the steamboat with it, and

had to pile a lot on the deck. Thus he could see
and enjoy as long as he could see, because the
appreciation of this favour had remained with him
to the last. You should have heard him say, 'My
ivory.' Oh, yes, I heard him. 'My Intended, my
ivory, my station, my river, my—' everything
belonged to him. It made me hold my breath in
expectation of hearing the wilderness burst into a
prodigious peal of laughter that would shake the
fixed stars in their places. Everything belonged to
him—but that was a trifle. The thing was to know
what he belonged to, how many powers of
darkness claimed him for their own. That was the
reflection that made you creepy all over. It was
impossible—it was not good for one either—trying
to imagine. He had taken a high seat amongst the
devils of the land—I mean literally. You can't
understand. How could you?—with solid pavement
under your feet, surrounded by kind neighbours
ready to cheer you or to fall on you, stepping
delicately between the butcher and the policeman,
in the holy terror of scandal and gallows and
lunatic asylums—how can you imagine what
particular region of the first ages a man's
untrammelled feet may take him into by the way of
solitude—utter solitude without a policeman—by
the way of silence—utter silence, where no

warning voice of a kind neighbour can be heard whispering of public opinion? These little things make all the great difference. When they are gone you must fall back upon your own innate strength, upon your own capacity for faithfulness. Of course you may be too much of a fool to go wrong—too dull even to know you are being assaulted by the powers of darkness. I take it, no fool ever made a bargain for his soul with the devil; the fool is too much of a fool, or the devil too much of a devil—I don't know which. Or you may be such a thunderingly exalted creature as to be altogether deaf and blind to anything but heavenly sights and sounds. Then the earth for you is only a standing place—and whether to be like this is your loss or your gain I won't pretend to say. But most of us are neither one nor the other. The earth for us is a place to live in, where we must put up with sights, with sounds, with smells, too, by Jove!—breathe dead hippo, so to speak, and not be contaminated. And there, don't you see? Your strength comes in, the faith in your ability for the digging of unostentatious holes to bury the stuff in—your power of devotion, not to yourself, but to an obscure, backbreaking business. And that's difficult enough. Mind, I am not trying to excuse or even explain—I am trying to account to myself for—for—Mr. Kurtz—for the shade of Mr. Kurtz. This initiated wraith from the back of Nowhere honoured me with its amazing confidence before it vanished altogether. This was because it could speak English to me. The original Kurtz had been educated partly in England, and—as he was good enough to say himself—his sympathies were in the right place. His mother was half-English, his father was half-French. All Europe contributed to the making of Kurtz; and by and by I learned that, most appropriately, the International Society for the Suppression of Savage Customs had intrusted him with the making of a report, for its future guidance. And he had written it, too. I've seen it. I've read it. It was eloquent, vibrating with eloquence, but too high-strung, I think. Seventeen pages of close writing he had found time for! But this must have been before his—let us say— nerves, went wrong, and caused him to preside at certain midnight dances ending with unspeakable rites, which—as far as I reluctantly gathered from what I heard at various times—were offered up to him—do you understand?—to Mr. Kurtz himself. But it was a beautiful piece of writing. The opening paragraph, however, in the light of later information, strikes me now as ominous. He began with the argument that we whites, from the point of development we had arrived at, 'must necessarily appear to them [savages] in the nature of supernatural beings—we approach them with the might as of a deity,' and so on, and so on. 'By the simple exercise of our will we can exert a power for good practically unbounded,' etc., etc. From that point he soared and took me with him. The peroration[8] was magnificent, though difficult to remember, you know. It gave me the notion of an exotic immensity ruled by an august benevolence. It made me tingle with enthusiasm. This was the unbounded power of eloquence—of words—of burning noble words. There were no practical hints to interrupt the magic current of phrases, unless a kind of note at the foot of the last page, scrawled evidently much later, in an unsteady hand, may be regarded as the exposition of a method. It was very simple, and at the end of that moving appeal to every altruistic sentiment it blazed at you, luminous and terrifying, like a flash of lightning in a serene sky: 'Exterminate all the brutes!' The curious part was that he had apparently forgotten all about that valuable postscriptum, because, later on, when he in a

---

[8] The conclusion (traditionally of a speech), an element of classical rhetoric with the purpose of summarizing the points and rousing the audience to agreement or action

sense came to himself, he repeatedly entreated me to take good care of 'my pamphlet' (he called it), as it was sure to have in the future a good influence upon his career. I had full information about all these things, and, besides, as it turned out, I was to have the care of his memory. I've done enough for it to give me the indisputable right to lay it, if I choose, for an everlasting rest in the dust-bin of progress, amongst all the sweepings and, figuratively speaking, all the dead cats of civilization. But then, you see, I can't choose. He won't be forgotten. Whatever he was, he was not common. He had the power to charm or frighten rudimentary souls into an aggravated witch-dance in his honour; he could also fill the small souls of the pilgrims with bitter misgivings: he had one devoted friend at least, and he had conquered one soul in the world that was neither rudimentary nor tainted with self-seeking. No; I can't forget him, though I am not prepared to affirm the fellow was exactly worth the life we lost in getting to him. I missed my late helmsman awfully—I missed him even while his body was still lying in the pilot-house. Perhaps you will think it passing strange this regret for a savage who was no more account than a grain of sand in a black Sahara. Well, don't you see, he had done something, he had steered;

for months I had him at my back—a help—an instrument. It was a kind of partnership. He steered for me—I had to look after him, I worried about his deficiencies, and thus a subtle bond had been created, of which I only became aware when it was suddenly broken. And the intimate profundity of that look he gave me when he received his hurt remains to this day in my memory—like a claim of distant kinship affirmed in a supreme moment.

"Poor fool! If he had only left that shutter alone. He had no restraint, no restraint—just like Kurtz—a tree swayed by the wind. As soon as I had put on a dry pair of slippers, I dragged him out, after first jerking the spear out of his side, which operation I confess I performed with my eyes shut tight. His heels leaped together over the little doorstep; his shoulders were pressed to my breast; I hugged him from behind desperately. Oh! he was heavy, heavy; heavier than any man on earth, I should imagine. Then without more ado I tipped him overboard. The current snatched him as though he had been a wisp of grass, and I saw the body roll over twice before I lost sight of it forever. All the pilgrims and the manager were then congregated on the awning-deck about the pilot-house, chattering at each other like a flock of excited magpies, and there was a scandalized murmur at my heartless promptitude. What they wanted to keep that body hanging about for I can't guess. Embalm it, maybe. But I had also heard another, and a very ominous, murmur on the deck below. My friends the wood-cutters were likewise scandalized, and with a better show of reason—though I admit that the reason itself was quite inadmissible. Oh, quite! I had made up my mind that if my late helmsman was to be eaten, the fishes alone should have him. He had been a very second-rate helmsman while alive, but now he was dead he might have become a first-class temptation, and possibly cause some startling trouble. Besides, I was anxious to take the wheel, the man in pink pajamas showing himself a hopeless duffer at the business.

"This I did directly the simple funeral was over. We were going half-speed, keeping right in the middle of the stream, and I listened to the talk about me. They had given up Kurtz, they had given up the station; Kurtz was dead, and the station had been burnt—and so on—and so on. The red-haired pilgrim was beside himself with the thought that at least this poor Kurtz had been properly avenged. 'Say! We must have made a glorious slaughter of them in the bush. Eh? What do you think? Say?' He positively danced, the bloodthirsty little gingery[9] beggar. And he had nearly fainted when he saw the wounded man! I could not help saying, 'You made a glorious lot of smoke, anyhow.' I had seen, from the way the tops of the bushes rustled and flew, that almost all the shots had gone too high. You can't hit anything unless you take aim and fire from the shoulder; but these chaps fired from the hip with their eyes shut. The retreat, I maintained—and I was right— was caused by the screeching of the steam whistle. Upon this they forgot Kurtz, and began to howl at me with indignant protests.

"The manager stood by the wheel murmuring confidentially about the necessity of getting well away down the river before dark at all events, when I saw in the distance a clearing on the riverside and the outlines of some sort of building. 'What's this?' I asked. He clapped his hands in wonder. 'The station!' he cried. I edged in at once, still going half-speed.

"Through my glasses I saw the slope of a hill interspersed with rare trees and perfectly free from undergrowth. A long decaying building on the summit was half buried in the high grass;

---

[9] Ginger (red) haired

the large holes in the peaked roof gaped black
from afar; the jungle and the woods made a
background. There was no enclosure or fence of
any kind; but there had been one apparently, for
near the house half-a-dozen slim posts remained
in a row, roughly trimmed, and with their upper
ends ornamented with round carved balls. The
rails, or whatever there had been between, had
disappeared. Of course the forest surrounded
all that. The river-bank was clear, and on the
waterside I saw a white man under a hat like
a cart-wheel beckoning persistently with his
whole arm. Examining the edge of the forest
above and below, I was almost certain I could
see movements—human forms gliding here and
there. I steamed past prudently, then stopped the
engines and let her drift down. The man on the
shore began to shout, urging us to land. 'We have
been attacked,' screamed the manager. 'I know—I
know. It's all right,' yelled back the other, as
cheerful as you please. 'Come along. It's all right. I
am glad.'

"His aspect reminded me of something I had
seen—something funny I had seen somewhere.
As I manoeuvred to get alongside, I was asking
myself, 'What does this fellow look like?' Suddenly

I got it. He looked like a harlequin.[10] His clothes
had been made of some stuff that was brown
holland probably, but it was covered with patches
all over, with bright patches, blue, red, and
yellow—patches on the back, patches on the front,
patches on elbows, on knees; coloured binding
around his jacket, scarlet edging at the bottom
of his trousers; and the sunshine made him
look extremely gay and wonderfully neat withal,
because you could see how beautifully all this
patching had been done. A beardless, boyish face,
very fair, no features to speak of, nose peeling,
little blue eyes, smiles and frowns chasing each
other over that open countenance like sunshine
and shadow on a wind-swept plain. 'Look out,
captain!' he cried; 'there's a snag lodged in here
last night.' What! Another snag? I confess I swore
shamefully. I had nearly holed my cripple, to
finish off that charming trip. The harlequin on
the bank turned his little pug-nose up to me. 'You
English?' he asked, all smiles. 'Are you?' I shouted
from the wheel. The smiles vanished, and he
shook his head as if sorry for my disappointment.

---

[10] A comic character, usually dressed in diamond-patterned
clothes (like the joker in a deck of cards); the description is
metaphorical here as later it says that his clothes are tattered
and patched.

Then he brightened up. 'Never mind!' he cried encouragingly. 'Are we in time?' I asked. 'He is up there,' he replied, with a toss of the head up the hill, and becoming gloomy all of a sudden. His face was like the autumn sky, overcast one moment and bright the next.

"When the manager, escorted by the pilgrims, all of them armed to the teeth, had gone to the house this chap came on board. 'I say, I don't like this. These natives are in the bush,' I said. He assured me earnestly it was all right. 'They are simple people,' he added; 'well, I am glad you came. It took me all my time to keep them off.' 'But you said it was all right,' I cried. 'Oh, they meant no harm,' he said; and as I stared he corrected himself, 'Not exactly.' Then vivaciously, 'My faith, your pilot-house wants a clean-up!' In the next breath he advised me to keep enough steam on the boiler to blow the whistle in case of any trouble. 'One good screech will do more for you than all your rifles. They are simple people,' he repeated. He rattled away at such a rate he quite overwhelmed me. He seemed to be trying to make up for lots of silence, and actually hinted, laughing, that such was the case. 'Don't you talk with Mr. Kurtz?' I said. 'You don't talk with that man—you listen to him,' he exclaimed with severe exaltation. 'But now—' He waved his arm, and in the twinkling of an eye was in the uttermost depths of despondency. In a moment he came up again with a jump, possessed himself of both my hands, shook them continuously, while he gabbled: 'Brother sailor . . . honour . . . pleasure . . . delight . . . introduce myself . . . Russian . . . son of an arch-priest . . . Government of Tambov . . .[11] What? Tobacco! English tobacco; the excellent English tobacco! Now, that's brotherly. Smoke? Where's a sailor that does not smoke?"

"The pipe soothed him, and gradually I made out he had run away from school, had gone to sea in a Russian ship; ran away again; served some time in English ships; was now reconciled with the arch-priest. He made a point of that. 'But when one is young one must see things, gather experience, ideas; enlarge the mind.' 'Here!' I interrupted. 'You can never tell! Here I met Mr. Kurtz,' he said, youthfully solemn and reproachful. I held my tongue after that. It appears he had persuaded a Dutch trading-house on the coast to fit him out with stores and goods, and had started for the interior with a light heart and no more idea of what would happen to him than a baby. He had

---

[11] A Russian city

been wandering about that river for nearly two years alone, cut off from everybody and everything. 'I am not so young as I look. I am twenty-five,' he said. 'At first old Van Shuyten would tell me to go to the devil,' he narrated with keen enjoyment; 'but I stuck to him, and talked and talked, till at last he got afraid I would talk the hind-leg off his favourite dog, so he gave me some cheap things and a few guns, and told me he hoped he would never see my face again. Good old Dutchman, Van Shuyten. I've sent him one small lot of ivory a year ago, so that he can't call me a little thief when I get back. I hope he got it. And for the rest I don't care. I had some wood stacked for you. That was my old house. Did you see?'

"I gave him Towson's book. He made as though he would kiss me, but restrained himself. 'The only book I had left, and I thought I had lost it,' he said, looking at it ecstatically. 'So many accidents happen to a man going about alone, you know. Canoes get upset sometimes—and sometimes you've got to clear out so quick when the people get angry.' He thumbed the pages. 'You made notes in Russian?' I asked. He nodded. 'I thought they were written in cipher,' I said. He laughed, then became serious. 'I had lots of trouble to keep these people off,' he said. 'Did they want to kill you?' I

asked. 'Oh, no!' he cried, and checked himself.
'Why did they attack us?' I pursued. He hesitated,
then said shamefacedly, 'They don't want him to
go.' 'Don't they?' I said curiously. He nodded a nod
full of mystery and wisdom. 'I tell you,' he cried,
'this man has enlarged my mind.' He opened his
arms wide, staring at me with his little blue eyes
that were perfectly round."

PART 2
REFLECTION QUESTIONS

1. Part 2 opens with Marlow learning more about Kurtz. What does he learn? Note in particular the report "that Kurtz had apparently intended to return himself, the station being by that time bare of goods and stores, but after coming three hundred miles, had suddenly decided to go back, which he started to do alone in a small dugout with four paddlers, leaving the half-caste to continue down the river with the ivory."

2. The manager of the Eldorado Expedition reports that Kurtz had said, "Each station should be like a beacon on the road towards better things, a centre for trade of course, but also for humanizing, improving, instructing." How do Kurtz's words compare to what others have said about the purposes of colonization? How do his words compare with what is actually going on?

3. Conrad's writing is dense and lyrical. Discuss the effect of the simile in the last part of this sentence: "In a few days the Eldorado Expedition went into the patient wilderness, that closed upon it as the sea closes over a diver." Examine other examples of Conrad's poetic writing.

4. What is evoked by Marlow's description of truth that is "stripped of its cloak of time"?

5. How does Marlow characterize the steamboat's fireman?

6. What does Marlow mean when he says, "The mind of man is capable of anything—because everything is in it, all the past as well as all the future"?

7. What is the significance of the reed hut and its contents that Marlow and his crew discover fifty miles below the Inner Station? How does the writing that looks like cipher (or code) reinforce the story's theme of the unknown and unknowable?

8. Consider other forms of communication that Marlow does not understand. Does the fact that he cannot decipher these forms of communication indicate that they have no meaning? Or something else?

9. How is Marlow's realization that the cannibals who are part of the crew have exercised great restraint significant to the theme of the work? Examine how racism is both implicit and questioned in this part of the story.

10. How does the attack on the steamboat from the shore take on different meaning later in the story? Why does Marlow assume, following the attack, that Kurtz would be dead?

11. What is the significance of Marlow's statement following the death of the helmsman that he was "morbidly anxious to change" his blood-soaked shoes and socks?

12. What kind of image of Kurtz is Marlow creating in his mind? Why is Marlow drawn to him?

13. When the crew is eight miles from Kurtz's compound, Marlow describes the jungle using imagery that makes the jungle seem alive. What are some words and phrases that achieve this? What is their effect?

14. What is the significance of the placement/context of the phrase "the heart of an impenetrable darkness" in this section?

15. Marlow dwells for a while on the absurdity of the entire situation. *Absurd* is an interesting word choice given its literal meaning, which is the lack of reason or rationality. How is this word, given its literal definition, a fitting one to describe the story?

16. What does Marlow mean when he tells his listeners, "You can't understand. How could you?—with solid pavement under your feet, surrounded by kind neighbors ready to cheer you or to fall on you, stepping delicately between the butcher and the policeman, in the holy terror of scandal and gallows and lunatic asylums—how can you

imagine what particular region of the first ages a man's untrammelled feet may take him into by the way of solitude—utter solitude without a police-man—by the way of silence—utter silence, where no warning voice of a kind neighbor can be heard whispering of public opinion? These little things make all the great difference"?

17. Marlow says, "I laid the ghost of his gifts at last with a lie," a part of the story that will be explained further in Part 3. Why might this hint of what Marlow does later fit well at this point in the narrative?

18. What does Marlow mean by this statement: "The earth for us is a place to live in, where we must put up with sights, with sounds, with smells, too, by Jove!—breathe dead hippo, so to speak, and not be contaminated"? How does this view both reflect and fall short of the gospel?

19. What is the significance of Marlow's assertion, "All Europe contributed to the making of Kurtz"?

20. What does Marlow learn about Kurtz by read-ing the report Kurtz created for the International Society for the Suppression of Savage Customs?

Why does Marlow dwell on the "eloquence" of
Kurtz's writing? What is the significance of the
postscript Kurtz makes to his report, which says,
"Exterminate all the brutes!"?

21. Note Marlow's description of Kurtz's compound
as he views it through his glasses (binoculars), in
particular the details of the posts, which Marlow
thinks are the remains of a fence.

22. The appearance of the Russian, or harlequin,
seems absurd (as defined above). How so? How
does his clothing contribute to this motif (a recur-
ring image or idea) of the absurd?

23. What does Marlow learn from the Russian
about the "cipher" written in the book he found at
the hut downriver? How might this understanding contribute to the developing theme in the story
about truth and meaning?

III

"I looked at him, lost in astonishment. There he was before me, in motley,[1] as though he had absconded from a troupe of mimes, enthusiastic, fabulous. His very existence was improbable, inexplicable, and altogether bewildering. He was an insoluble problem. It was inconceivable how he had existed, how he had succeeded in getting so far, how he had managed to remain—why he did not instantly disappear. 'I went a little farther,' he said, 'then still a little farther—till I had gone so far that

---

[1] Patched, variegated appearance

I don't know how I'll ever get back. Never mind.
Plenty time. I can manage. You take Kurtz away
quick—quick—I tell you.' The glamour of youth
enveloped his parti-coloured rags, his destitution,
his loneliness, the essential desolation of his
futile wanderings. For months—for years—his
life hadn't been worth a day's purchase; and
there he was gallantly, thoughtlessly alive, to all
appearances indestructible solely by the virtue of
his few years and of his unreflecting audacity. I
was seduced into something like admiration—like
envy. Glamour urged him on, glamour kept him
unscathed. He surely wanted nothing from the
wilderness but space to breathe in and to push
on through. His need was to exist, and to move
onwards at the greatest possible risk, and with
a maximum of privation. If the absolutely pure,
uncalculating, unpractical spirit of adventure had
ever ruled a human being, it ruled this bepatched
youth. I almost envied him the possession of
this modest and clear flame. It seemed to have
consumed all thought of self so completely, that
even while he was talking to you, you forgot that
it was he—the man before your eyes—who had
gone through these things. I did not envy him his
devotion to Kurtz, though. He had not meditated
over it. It came to him, and he accepted it with

a sort of eager fatalism. I must say that to me it appeared about the most dangerous thing in every way he had come upon so far.

"They had come together unavoidably, like two ships becalmed near each other, and lay rubbing sides at last. I suppose Kurtz wanted an audience, because on a certain occasion, when encamped in the forest, they had talked all night, or more probably Kurtz had talked. 'We talked of everything,' he said, quite transported at the recollection. 'I forgot there was such a thing as sleep. The night did not seem to last an hour. Everything! Everything! . . . Of love, too.' 'Ah, he talked to you of love!' I said, much amused. 'It isn't what you think,' he cried, almost passionately. 'It was in general. He made me see things—things.'

"He threw his arms up. We were on deck at the time, and the headman of my wood-cutters, lounging near by, turned upon him his heavy and glittering eyes. I looked around, and I don't know why, but I assure you that never, never before, did this land, this river, this jungle, the very arch of this blazing sky, appear to me so hopeless and so dark, so impenetrable to human thought, so pitiless to human weakness. 'And, ever since, you have been with him, of course?' I said.

"On the contrary. It appears their intercourse had been very much broken by various causes. He had, as he informed me proudly, managed to nurse Kurtz through two illnesses (he alluded to it as you would to some risky feat), but as a rule Kurtz wandered alone, far in the depths of the forest. 'Very often coming to this station, I had to wait days and days before he would turn up,' he said. 'Ah, it was worth waiting for!—sometimes.' 'What was he doing? Exploring or what?' I asked. 'Oh, yes, of course'; he had discovered lots of villages, a lake, too—he did not know exactly in what direction; it was dangerous to inquire too much—but mostly his expeditions had been for ivory. 'But he had no goods to trade with by that time,' I objected. 'There's a good lot of cartridges left even yet,' he answered, looking away. 'To speak plainly, he raided the country,' I said. He nodded. 'Not alone, surely!' He muttered something about the villages round that lake. 'Kurtz got the tribe to follow him, did he?' I suggested. He fidgeted a little. 'They adored him,' he said. The tone of these words was so extraordinary that I looked at him searchingly. It was curious to see his mingled eagerness and reluctance to speak of Kurtz. The man filled his life, occupied his thoughts, swayed his emotions. 'What can you expect?' he burst out; 'he came to them with thunder and lightning, you know—and they had never seen anything like it—and very terrible. He could be very terrible. You can't judge Mr. Kurtz as you would an ordinary man. No, no, no! Now—just to give you an idea—I don't mind telling you, he wanted to shoot me, too, one day—but I don't judge him.' 'Shoot you!' I cried. 'What for?' 'Well, I had a small lot of ivory the chief of that village near my house gave me. You see I used to shoot game for them. Well, he wanted it, and wouldn't hear reason. He declared he would shoot me unless I gave him the ivory and then cleared out of the country, because he could do so, and had a fancy for it, and there was nothing on earth to prevent him killing whom he jolly well pleased. And it was true, too. I gave him the ivory. What did I care! But I didn't clear out. No, no. I couldn't leave him. I had to be careful, of course, till we got friendly again for a time. He had his second illness then. Afterwards I had to keep out of the way; but I didn't mind. He was living for the most part in those villages on the lake. When he came down to the river, sometimes he would take to me, and sometimes it was better for me to be careful. This man suffered too much. He hated all this, and somehow he couldn't get away. When I had a chance I begged him to try and leave while there was time; I offered to go back with him. And he would say yes, and then he would remain; go off on another ivory hunt; disappear for weeks; forget himself amongst these people— forget himself—you know.' 'Why! He's mad,' I said. He protested indignantly. Mr. Kurtz couldn't be mad. If I had heard him talk, only two days ago, I wouldn't dare hint at such a thing. . . . I had taken up my binoculars while we talked, and was looking at the shore, sweeping the limit of the forest at each side and at the back of the house. The consciousness of there being people in that bush, so silent, so quiet—as silent and quiet as the ruined house on the hill—made me uneasy. There was no sign on the face of nature of this amazing tale that was not so much told as suggested to me in desolate exclamations, completed by shrugs, in interrupted phrases, in hints ending in deep sighs. The woods were unmoved, like a mask—heavy, like the closed door of a prison—they looked with their air of hidden knowledge, of patient expectation, of unapproachable silence. The Russian was explaining to me that it was only lately that Mr. Kurtz had come down to the river, bringing along with him all the fighting men of that lake tribe. He had been absent for several months—getting himself adored, I suppose—and had come down

unexpectedly, with the intention to all appearance
of making a raid either across the river or down
stream. Evidently the appetite for more ivory
had got the better of the—what shall I say?—
less material aspirations. However he had got
much worse suddenly. 'I heard he was lying here
helpless, and so I came up—took my chance,' said
the Russian. 'Oh, he is bad, very bad.' I directed
my glass[2] to the house. There were no signs of
life, but there was the ruined roof, the long mud
walls peeping above the grass, with three little
square window-holes, no two of the same size;
all this brought within reach of my hand, as it
were. And then I made a brusque movement, and
one of the remaining posts of that vanished fence
leaped up in the field of my glass. You remember
I told you I had been struck at the distance
by certain attempts at ornamentation, rather
remarkable in the ruinous aspect of the place.
Now I had suddenly a nearer view, and its first
result was to make me throw my head back as if
before a blow. Then I went carefully from post to
post with my glass, and I saw my mistake. These
round knobs were not ornamental but symbolic;
they were expressive and puzzling, striking and

---

[2] His binoculars

disturbing—food for thought and also for vultures if there had been any looking down from the sky; but at all events for such ants as were industrious enough to ascend the pole. They would have been even more impressive, those heads on the stakes, if their faces had not been turned to the house. Only one, the first I had made out, was facing my way. I was not so shocked as you may think. The start back I had given was really nothing but a movement of surprise. I had expected to see a knob of wood there, you know. I returned deliberately to the first I had seen—and there it was, black, dried, sunken, with closed eyelids—a head that seemed to sleep at the top of that pole, and, with the shrunken dry lips showing a narrow white line of the teeth, was smiling, too, smiling continuously at some endless and jocose dream of that eternal slumber.

"I am not disclosing any trade secrets. In fact, the manager said afterwards that Mr. Kurtz's methods had ruined the district. I have no opinion on that point, but I want you clearly to understand that there was nothing exactly profitable in these heads being there. They only showed that Mr. Kurtz lacked restraint in the gratification of his various lusts, that there was something wanting in him—some small matter which, when the pressing need arose, could not be found under his magnificent eloquence. Whether he knew of this deficiency himself I can't say. I think the knowledge came to him at last—only at the very last. But the wilderness had found him out early, and had taken on him a terrible vengeance for the fantastic invasion. I think it had whispered to him things about himself which he did not know, things of which he had no conception till he took counsel with this great solitude—and the whisper had proved irresistibly fascinating. It echoed loudly within him because he was hollow at the core. . . . I put down the glass, and the head that had appeared near enough to be spoken to seemed at once to have leaped away from me into inaccessible distance.

"The admirer of Mr. Kurtz was a bit crestfallen. In a hurried, indistinct voice he began to assure me he had not dared to take these—say, symbols— down. He was not afraid of the natives; they would not stir till Mr. Kurtz gave the word. His ascendancy was extraordinary. The camps of these people surrounded the place, and the chiefs came every day to see him. They would crawl. . . . 'I don't want to know anything of the ceremonies used when approaching Mr. Kurtz,' I shouted. Curious, this feeling that came over me that such details

would be more intolerable than those heads drying
on the stakes under Mr. Kurtz's windows. After
all, that was only a savage sight, while I seemed
at one bound to have been transported into some
lightless region of subtle horrors, where pure,
uncomplicated savagery was a positive relief, being
something that had a right to exist—obviously—in
the sunshine. The young man looked at me with
surprise. I suppose it did not occur to him that Mr.
Kurtz was no idol of mine. He forgot I hadn't heard
any of these splendid monologues on, what was it?
on love, justice, conduct of life—or what not. If it
had come to crawling before Mr. Kurtz, he crawled
as much as the veriest[3] savage of them all. I had
no idea of the conditions, he said: these heads
were the heads of rebels. I shocked him excessively
by laughing. Rebels! What would be the next
definition I was to hear? There had been enemies,
criminals, workers—and these were rebels. Those
rebellious heads looked very subdued to me on
their sticks. 'You don't know how such a life tries
a man like Kurtz,' cried Kurtz's last disciple. 'Well,
and you?' I said. 'I! I! I am a simple man. I have no
great thoughts. I want nothing from anybody. How
can you compare me to. . . ?' His feelings were too

---

[3] Extreme or exceedingly

much for speech, and suddenly he broke down.
'I don't understand,' he groaned. 'I've been doing
my best to keep him alive, and that's enough. I
had no hand in all this. I have no abilities. There
hasn't been a drop of medicine or a mouthful of
invalid food for months here. He was shamefully
abandoned. A man like this, with such ideas.
Shamefully! Shamefully! I—I—haven't slept for the
last ten nights . . .'

"His voice lost itself in the calm of the evening.
The long shadows of the forest had slipped
downhill while we talked, had gone far beyond
the ruined hovel, beyond the symbolic row of
stakes. All this was in the gloom, while we down
there were yet in the sunshine, and the stretch
of the river abreast of the clearing glittered in a
still and dazzling splendour, with a murky and
overshadowed bend above and below. Not a living
soul was seen on the shore. The bushes did not
rustle.

"Suddenly round the corner of the house
a group of men appeared, as though they had
come up from the ground. They waded waist-
deep in the grass, in a compact body, bearing an
improvised stretcher in their midst. Instantly, in
the emptiness of the landscape, a cry arose whose
shrillness pierced the still air like a sharp arrow

flying straight to the very heart of the land; and, as
if by enchantment, streams of human beings—of
naked human beings—with spears in their hands,
with bows, with shields, with wild glances and
savage movements, were poured into the clearing
by the dark-faced and pensive forest. The bushes
shook, the grass swayed for a time, and then
everything stood still in attentive immobility.

"'Now, if he does not say the right thing to them
we are all done for,' said the Russian at my elbow.
The knot of men with the stretcher had stopped,
too, halfway to the steamer, as if petrified. I saw
the man on the stretcher sit up, lank and with an
uplifted arm, above the shoulders of the bearers.
'Let us hope that the man who can talk so well of
love in general will find some particular reason
to spare us this time,' I said. I resented bitterly
the absurd danger of our situation, as if to be at
the mercy of that atrocious phantom had been
a dishonouring necessity. I could not hear a
sound, but through my glasses I saw the thin arm
extended commandingly, the lower jaw moving,
the eyes of that apparition shining darkly far in
its bony head that nodded with grotesque jerks.
Kurtz—Kurtz—that means short in German—don't
it? Well, the name was as true as everything else
in his life—and death. He looked at least seven

feet long. His covering had fallen off, and his body emerged from it pitiful and appalling as from a winding-sheet. I could see the cage of his ribs all astir, the bones of his arm waving. It was as though an animated image of death carved out of old ivory had been shaking its hand with menaces at a motionless crowd of men made of dark and glittering bronze. I saw him open his mouth wide—it gave him a weirdly voracious aspect, as though he had wanted to swallow all the air, all the earth, all the men before him. A deep voice reached me faintly. He must have been shouting. He fell back suddenly. The stretcher shook as the bearers staggered forward again, and almost at the same time I noticed that the crowd of savages was vanishing without any perceptible movement of retreat, as if the forest that had ejected these beings so suddenly had drawn them in again as the breath is drawn in a long aspiration.

"Some of the pilgrims behind the stretcher carried his arms—two shot-guns, a heavy rifle, and a light revolver-carbine—the thunderbolts of that pitiful Jupiter. The manager bent over him murmuring as he walked beside his head. They laid him down in one of the little cabins—just a room for a bed place and a camp-stool or two, you know. We had brought his belated correspondence, and a lot of torn envelopes and open letters littered his bed. His hand roamed feebly amongst these papers. I was struck by the fire of his eyes and the composed languor of his expression. It was not so much the exhaustion of disease. He did not seem in pain. This shadow looked satiated and calm, as though for the moment it had had its fill of all the emotions.

"He rustled one of the letters, and looking straight in my face said, 'I am glad.' Somebody had been writing to him about me. These special recommendations were turning up again. The volume of tone he emitted without effort, almost without the trouble of moving his lips, amazed me. A voice! A voice! It was grave, profound, vibrating, while the man did not seem capable of a whisper. However, he had enough strength in him— factitious no doubt—to very nearly make an end of us, as you shall hear directly.

"The manager appeared silently in the doorway; I stepped out at once and he drew the curtain after me. The Russian, eyed curiously by the pilgrims, was staring at the shore. I followed the direction of his glance.

"Dark human shapes could be made out in the distance, flitting indistinctly against the gloomy border of the forest, and near the river two bronze figures, leaning on tall spears, stood in the sunlight under fantastic head-dresses of spotted skins, warlike and still in statuesque repose. And from right to left along the lighted shore moved a wild and gorgeous apparition of a woman.

"She walked with measured steps, draped in striped and fringed cloths, treading the earth proudly, with a slight jingle and flash of barbarous ornaments. She carried her head high; her hair was done in the shape of a helmet; she had brass leggings to the knee, brass wire gauntlets to the elbow, a crimson spot on her tawny check, innumerable necklaces of glass beads on her neck; bizarre things, charms, gifts of witch-men, that hung about her, glittered and trembled at every step. She must have had the value of several elephant tusks upon her. She was savage and superb, wild-eyed and magnificent; there was something ominous and stately in her deliberate progress. And in the hush that had fallen suddenly upon the whole sorrowful land, the immense wilderness, the colossal body of the fecund and mysterious life seemed to look at her, pensive, as though it had been looking at the image of its own tenebrous[4] and passionate soul.

---

[4] Dark, murky, or obscure

"She came abreast of the steamer, stood still, and faced us. Her long shadow fell to the water's edge. Her face had a tragic and fierce aspect of wild sorrow and of dumb pain mingled with the fear of some struggling, half-shaped resolve. She stood looking at us without a stir, and like the wilderness itself, with an air of brooding over an inscrutable purpose. A whole minute passed, and then she made a step forward. There was a low jingle, a glint of yellow metal, a sway of fringed draperies, and she stopped as if her heart had failed her. The young fellow by my side growled. The pilgrims murmured at my back. She looked at us all as if her life had depended upon the unswerving steadiness of her glance. Suddenly she opened her bared arms and threw them up rigid above her head, as though in an uncontrollable desire to touch the sky, and at the same time the swift shadows darted out on the earth, swept around on the river, gathering the steamer into a shadowy embrace. A formidable silence hung over the scene.

"She turned away slowly, walked on, following the bank, and passed into the bushes to the left. Once only her eyes gleamed back at us in the dusk of the thickets before she disappeared.

"'If she had offered to come aboard I really think I would have tried to shoot her,' said the man of patches, nervously. 'I have been risking my life every day for the last fortnight to keep her out of the house. She got in one day and kicked up a row about those miserable rags I picked up in the storeroom to mend my clothes with. I wasn't decent. At least it must have been that, for she talked like a fury to Kurtz for an hour, pointing at me now and then. I don't understand the dialect of this tribe. Luckily for me, I fancy Kurtz felt too ill that day to care, or there would have been mischief. I don't understand. . . . No—it's too much for me. Ah, well, it's all over now.'

"At this moment I heard Kurtz's deep voice behind the curtain: 'Save me!—save the ivory, you mean. Don't tell me. Save *me*! Why, I've had to save you. You are interrupting my plans now. Sick! Sick! Not so sick as you would like to believe. Never mind. I'll carry my ideas out yet—I will return. I'll show you what can be done. You with your little peddling notions—you are interfering with me. I will return. I . . .'

"The manager came out. He did me the honour to take me under the arm and lead me aside. 'He is very low, very low,' he said. He considered it necessary to sigh, but neglected to be consistently

sorrowful. 'We have done all we could for him—
haven't we? But there is no disguising the fact,
Mr. Kurtz has done more harm than good to the
Company. He did not see the time was not ripe for
vigorous action. Cautiously, cautiously—that's my
principle. We must be cautious yet. The district
is closed to us for a time. Deplorable! Upon the
whole, the trade will suffer. I don't deny there
is a remarkable quantity of ivory—mostly fossil.
We must save it, at all events—but look how
precarious the position is—and why? Because the
method is unsound.' 'Do you,' said I, looking at the
shore, 'call it "unsound method?"' 'Without doubt,'
he exclaimed hotly. 'Don't you?'. . . 'No method
at all,' I murmured after a while. 'Exactly,' he
exulted. 'I anticipated this. Shows a complete want
of judgment. It is my duty to point it out in the
proper quarter.' 'Oh,' said I, 'that fellow—what's
his name?—the brickmaker, will make a readable
report for you.' He appeared confounded for a
moment. It seemed to me I had never breathed
an atmosphere so vile, and I turned mentally to
Kurtz for relief—positively for relief. 'Nevertheless
I think Mr. Kurtz is a remarkable man,' I said with
emphasis. He started, dropped on me a cold heavy
glance, said very quietly, 'he *was*,' and turned his
back on me. My hour of favour was over; I found

myself lumped along with Kurtz as a partisan of methods for which the time was not ripe: I was unsound! Ah! but it was something to have at least a choice of nightmares.

"I had turned to the wilderness really, not to Mr. Kurtz, who, I was ready to admit, was as good as buried. And for a moment it seemed to me as if I also were buried in a vast grave full of unspeakable secrets. I felt an intolerable weight oppressing my breast, the smell of the damp earth, the unseen presence of victorious corruption, the darkness of an impenetrable night. . . . The Russian tapped me on the shoulder. I heard him mumbling and stammering something about 'brother seaman—couldn't conceal—knowledge of matters that would affect Mr. Kurtz's reputation.' I waited. For him evidently Mr. Kurtz was not in his grave; I suspect that for him Mr. Kurtz was one of the immortals. 'Well!' said I at last, 'speak out. As it happens, I am Mr. Kurtz's friend—in a way.'

"He stated with a good deal of formality that had we not been 'of the same profession,' he would have kept the matter to himself without regard to consequences. 'He suspected there was an active ill-will towards him on the part of these white men that—' 'You are right,' I said, remembering a certain conversation I had overheard. 'The manager thinks you ought to be hanged.' He showed a concern at this intelligence which amused me at first. 'I had better get out of the way quietly,' he said earnestly. 'I can do no more for Kurtz now, and they would soon find some excuse. What's to stop them? There's a military post three hundred miles from here.' 'Well, upon my word,' said I, 'perhaps you had better go if you have any friends amongst the savages near by.' 'Plenty,' he said. 'They are simple people—and I want nothing, you know.' He stood biting his lip, then: 'I don't want any harm to happen to these whites here, but of course I was thinking of Mr. Kurtz's reputation—but you are a brother seaman and—' 'All right,' said I, after a time. 'Mr. Kurtz's reputation is safe with me.' I did not know how truly I spoke.

"He informed me, lowering his voice, that it was Kurtz who had ordered the attack to be made on the steamer. 'He hated sometimes the idea of being taken away—and then again. . . . But I don't understand these matters. I am a simple man. He thought it would scare you away—that you would give it up, thinking him dead. I could not stop him. Oh, I had an awful time of it this last month.' 'Very well,' I said. 'He is all right now.' 'Ye-e-es,' he muttered, not very convinced apparently.

'Thanks,' said I; 'I shall keep my eyes open.' 'But quiet-eh?' he urged anxiously. 'It would be awful for his reputation if anybody here—' I promised a complete discretion with great gravity. 'I have a canoe and three black fellows waiting not very far. I am off. Could you give me a few Martini-Henry cartridges?' I could, and did, with proper secrecy. He helped himself, with a wink at me, to a handful of my tobacco. 'Between sailors—you know—good English tobacco.' At the door of the pilot-house he turned round—'I say, haven't you a pair of shoes you could spare?' He raised one leg. 'Look.' The soles were tied with knotted strings sandalwise under his bare feet. I rooted out an old pair, at which he looked with admiration before tucking it under his left arm. One of his pockets (bright red) was bulging with cartridges, from the other (dark blue) peeped 'Towson's Inquiry,' etc., etc. He seemed to think himself excellently well equipped for a renewed encounter with the wilderness. 'Ah! I'll never, never meet such a man again. You ought to have heard him recite poetry—his own, too, it was, he told me. Poetry!' He rolled his eyes at the recollection of these delights. 'Oh, he enlarged my mind!' 'Good-bye,' said I. He shook hands and vanished in the night. Sometimes I ask myself

whether I had ever really seen him—whether it
was possible to meet such a phenomenon! . . .

"When I woke up shortly after midnight his
warning came to my mind with its hint of danger
that seemed, in the starred darkness, real enough
to make me get up for the purpose of having a look
round. On the hill a big fire burned, illuminating
fitfully a crooked corner of the station-house. One
of the agents with a picket of a few of our blacks,
armed for the purpose, was keeping guard over
the ivory; but deep within the forest, red gleams
that wavered, that seemed to sink and rise from
the ground amongst confused columnar shapes
of intense blackness, showed the exact position of
the camp where Mr. Kurtz's adorers were keeping
their uneasy vigil. The monotonous beating of a
big drum filled the air with muffled shocks and
a lingering vibration. A steady droning sound of
many men chanting each to himself some weird
incantation came out from the black, flat wall
of the woods as the humming of bees comes
out of a hive, and had a strange narcotic effect
upon my half-awake senses. I believe I dozed
off leaning over the rail, till an abrupt burst of
yells, an overwhelming outbreak of a pent-up and
mysterious frenzy, woke me up in a bewildered
wonder. It was cut short all at once, and the low

droning went on with an effect of audible and soothing silence. I glanced casually into the little cabin. A light was burning within, but Mr. Kurtz was not there.

"I think I would have raised an outcry if I had believed my eyes. But I didn't believe them at first—the thing seemed so impossible. The fact is I was completely unnerved by a sheer blank fright, pure abstract terror, unconnected with any distinct shape of physical danger. What made this emotion so overpowering was—how shall I define it?—the moral shock I received, as if something altogether monstrous, intolerable to thought and odious to the soul, had been thrust upon me unexpectedly. This lasted of course the merest fraction of a second, and then the usual sense of commonplace, deadly danger, the possibility of a sudden onslaught and massacre, or something of the kind, which I saw impending, was positively welcome and composing. It pacified me, in fact, so much that I did not raise an alarm.

"There was an agent buttoned up inside an ulster[5] and sleeping on a chair on deck within three feet of me. The yells had not awakened him; he snored very slightly; I left him to his slumbers

---

[5] A long, loose overcoat

and leaped ashore. I did not betray Mr. Kurtz—it
was ordered I should never betray him—it was
written I should be loyal to the nightmare of my
choice. I was anxious to deal with this shadow
by myself alone—and to this day I don't know
why I was so jealous of sharing with any one the
peculiar blackness of that experience.

"As soon as I got on the bank I saw a trail—a
broad trail through the grass. I remember the
exultation with which I said to myself, 'He can't
walk—he is crawling on all-fours—I've got him.'
The grass was wet with dew. I strode rapidly with
clenched fists. I fancy I had some vague notion
of falling upon him and giving him a drubbing. I
don't know. I had some imbecile thoughts. The
knitting old woman with the cat obtruded herself
upon my memory as a most improper person to
be sitting at the other end of such an affair. I saw
a row of pilgrims squirting lead in the air out of
Winchesters held to the hip. I thought I would
never get back to the steamer, and imagined
myself living alone and unarmed in the woods to
an advanced age. Such silly things—you know.
And I remember I confounded the beat of the drum
with the beating of my heart, and was pleased at
its calm regularity.

"I kept to the track though—then stopped to listen. The night was very clear; a dark blue space, sparkling with dew and starlight, in which black things stood very still. I thought I could see a kind of motion ahead of me. I was strangely cocksure of everything that night. I actually left the track and ran in a wide semicircle (I verily believe chuckling to myself) so as to get in front of that stir, of that motion I had seen—if indeed I had seen anything. I was circumventing Kurtz as though it had been a boyish game.

"I came upon him, and, if he had not heard me coming, I would have fallen over him, too, but he got up in time. He rose, unsteady, long, pale, indistinct, like a vapour exhaled by the earth, and swayed slightly, misty and silent before me; while at my back the fires loomed between the trees, and the murmur of many voices issued from the forest. I had cut him off cleverly; but when actually confronting him I seemed to come to my senses, I saw the danger in its right proportion. It was by no means over yet. Suppose he began to shout? Though he could hardly stand, there was still plenty of vigour in his voice. 'Go away—hide yourself,' he said, in that profound tone. It was very awful. I glanced back. We were within thirty yards from the nearest fire. A black figure stood up, strode on long black legs, waving long black arms, across the glow. It had horns—antelope horns, I think—on its head. Some sorcerer, some witch-man, no doubt: it looked fiendlike enough. 'Do you know what you are doing?' I whispered. 'Perfectly,' he answered, raising his voice for that single word: it sounded to me far off and yet loud, like a hail through a speaking-trumpet. 'If he makes a row we are lost,' I thought to myself. This clearly was not a case for fisticuffs, even apart from the very natural aversion I had to beat that Shadow—this wandering and tormented thing. 'You will be lost,' I said—'utterly lost.' One gets sometimes such a flash of inspiration, you know. I did say the right thing, though indeed he could not have been more irretrievably lost than he was at this very moment, when the foundations of our intimacy were being laid—to endure—to endure— even to the end—even beyond.

"'I had immense plans,' he muttered irresolutely. 'Yes,' said I; 'but if you try to shout I'll smash your head with—' There was not a stick or a stone near. 'I will throttle you for good,' I corrected myself. 'I was on the threshold of great things,' he pleaded, in a voice of longing, with a wistfulness of tone that made my blood run cold. 'And now for this stupid scoundrel—' 'Your success

190

in Europe is assured in any case,' I affirmed steadily. I did not want to have the throttling of him, you understand—and indeed it would have been very little use for any practical purpose. I tried to break the spell—the heavy, mute spell of the wilderness—that seemed to draw him to its pitiless breast by the awakening of forgotten and brutal instincts, by the memory of gratified and monstrous passions. This alone, I was convinced, had driven him out to the edge of the forest, to the bush, towards the gleam of fires, the throb of drums, the drone of weird incantations; this alone had beguiled his unlawful soul beyond the bounds of permitted aspirations. And, don't you see, the terror of the position was not in being knocked on the head—though I had a very lively sense of that danger, too—but in this, that I had to deal with a being to whom I could not appeal in the name of anything high or low. I had, even like the natives, to invoke him—himself—his own exalted and incredible degradation. There was nothing either above or below him, and I knew it. He had kicked himself loose of the earth. Confound the man! He had kicked the very earth to pieces. He was alone, and I before him did not know whether I stood on the ground or floated in the air. I've been telling you what we said—repeating the phrases

we pronounced—but what's the good? They were
common everyday words—the familiar, vague
sounds exchanged on every waking day of life.
But what of that? They had behind them, to my
mind, the terrific suggestiveness of words heard in
dreams, of phrases spoken in nightmares. Soul!
If anybody ever struggled with a soul, I am the
man. And I wasn't arguing with a lunatic either.
Believe me or not, his intelligence was perfectly
clear—concentrated, it is true, upon himself with
horrible intensity, yet clear; and therein was
my only chance—barring, of course, the killing
him there and then, which wasn't so good, on
account of unavoidable noise. But his soul was
mad. Being alone in the wilderness, it had looked
within itself, and, by heavens! I tell you, it had
gone mad. I had—for my sins, I suppose—to go
through the ordeal of looking into it myself. No
eloquence could have been so withering to one's
belief in mankind as his final burst of sincerity. He
struggled with himself, too. I saw it—I heard it. I
saw the inconceivable mystery of a soul that knew
no restraint, no faith, and no fear, yet struggling
blindly with itself. I kept my head pretty well; but
when I had him at last stretched on the couch,
I wiped my forehead, while my legs shook under
me as though I had carried half a ton on my back

down that hill. And yet I had only supported him, his bony arm clasped round my neck—and he was not much heavier than a child.

"When next day we left at noon, the crowd, of whose presence behind the curtain of trees I had been acutely conscious all the time, flowed out of the woods again, filled the clearing, covered the slope with a mass of naked, breathing, quivering, bronze bodies. I steamed up a bit, then swung down stream, and two thousand eyes followed the evolutions of the splashing, thumping, fierce river-demon beating the water with its terrible tail and breathing black smoke into the air. In front of the first rank, along the river, three men, plastered with bright red earth from head to foot, strutted to and fro restlessly. When we came abreast again, they faced the river, stamped their feet, nodded their horned heads, swayed their scarlet bodies; they shook towards the fierce river-demon a bunch of black feathers, a mangy skin with a pendent tail—something that looked a dried gourd; they shouted periodically together strings of amazing words that resembled no sounds of human language; and the deep murmurs of the crowd, interrupted suddenly, were like the responses of some satanic litany.

"We had carried Kurtz into the pilot-house: there was more air there. Lying on the couch, he stared through the open shutter. There was an eddy in the mass of human bodies, and the woman with helmeted head and tawny cheeks rushed out to the very brink of the stream. She put out her hands, shouted something, and all that wild mob took up the shout in a roaring chorus of articulated, rapid, breathless utterance.

"'Do you understand this?' I asked.

"He kept on looking out past me with fiery, longing eyes, with a mingled expression of wistfulness and hate. He made no answer, but I saw a smile, a smile of indefinable meaning, appear on his colourless lips that a moment after twitched convulsively. 'Do I not?' he said slowly, gasping, as if the words had been torn out of him by a supernatural power.

"I pulled the string of the whistle, and I did this because I saw the pilgrims on deck getting out their rifles with an air of anticipating a jolly lark. At the sudden screech there was a movement of abject terror through that wedged mass of bodies. 'Don't! don't you frighten them away,' cried some one on deck disconsolately. I pulled the string time after time. They broke and ran, they leaped, they crouched, they swerved, they dodged the flying terror of the sound. The three red chaps had fallen flat, face down on the shore, as though they had been shot dead. Only the barbarous and superb woman did not so much as flinch, and stretched tragically her bare arms after us over the sombre and glittering river.

"And then that imbecile crowd down on the deck started their little fun, and I could see nothing more for smoke.

"The brown current ran swiftly out of the heart of darkness, bearing us down towards the sea with twice the speed of our upward progress; and Kurtz's life was running swiftly, too, ebbing, ebbing out of his heart into the sea of inexorable time. The manager was very placid, he had no vital anxieties now, he took us both in with a comprehensive and satisfied glance: the 'affair' had come off as well as could be wished. I saw the time approaching when I would be left alone of the party of 'unsound method.' The pilgrims looked upon me with disfavour. I was, so to speak, numbered with the dead. It is strange how I accepted this unforeseen partnership, this choice of nightmares forced upon me in the tenebrous land invaded by these mean and greedy phantoms.

"Kurtz discoursed. A voice! a voice! It rang deep to the very last. It survived his strength to

hide in the magnificent folds of eloquence the
barren darkness of his heart. Oh, he struggled!
He struggled! The wastes of his weary brain
were haunted by shadowy images now—images
of wealth and fame revolving obsequiously
round his unextinguishable gift of noble and
lofty expression. My Intended, my station, my
career, my ideas—these were the subjects for the
occasional utterances of elevated sentiments. The
shade of the original Kurtz frequented the bedside
of the hollow sham, whose fate it was to be buried
presently in the mould[6] of primeval earth. But
both the diabolic love and the unearthly hate of
the mysteries it had penetrated fought for the
possession of that soul satiated with primitive
emotions, avid of lying fame, of sham distinction,
of all the appearances of success and power.

"Sometimes he was contemptibly childish. He
desired to have kings meet him at railway-stations
on his return from some ghastly Nowhere, where
he intended to accomplish great things. 'You show
them you have in you something that is really
profitable, and then there will be no limits to
the recognition of your ability,' he would say. 'Of
course you must take care of the motives—right

---

[6] Dirt, soil

motives—always.' The long reaches that were like one and the same reach, monotonous bends that were exactly alike, slipped past the steamer with their multitude of secular[7] trees looking patiently after this grimy fragment of another world, the forerunner of change, of conquest, of trade, of massacres, of blessings. I looked ahead—piloting. 'Close the shutter,' said Kurtz suddenly one day; 'I can't bear to look at this.' I did so. There was a silence. 'Oh, but I will wring your heart yet!' he cried at the invisible wilderness.

"We broke down—as I had expected—and had to lie up for repairs at the head of an island. This delay was the first thing that shook Kurtz's confidence. One morning he gave me a packet of papers and a photograph—the lot tied together with a shoe-string. 'Keep this for me,' he said. 'This noxious fool' (meaning the manager) 'is capable of prying into my boxes when I am not looking.' In the afternoon I saw him. He was lying on his back with closed eyes, and I withdrew quietly, but I heard him mutter, 'Live rightly, die, die . . .' I listened. There was nothing more. Was he rehearsing some speech in his sleep, or was

---

[7] Old, ancient (from the meaning of *secular* as relating to temporality)

it a fragment of a phrase from some newspaper article? He had been writing for the papers and meant to do so again, 'for the furthering of my ideas. It's a duty.'

"His was an impenetrable darkness. I looked at him as you peer down at a man who is lying at the bottom of a precipice where the sun never shines. But I had not much time to give him, because I was helping the engine-driver to take to pieces the leaky cylinders, to straighten a bent connecting-rod, and in other such matters. I lived in an infernal mess of rust, filings, nuts, bolts, spanners, hammers, ratchet-drills—things I abominate, because I don't get on with them. I tended the little forge we fortunately had aboard; I toiled wearily in a wretched scrap heap—unless I had the shakes too bad to stand.

"One evening coming in with a candle I was startled to hear him say a little tremulously, 'I am lying here in the dark waiting for death.' The light was within a foot of his eyes. I forced myself to murmur, 'Oh, nonsense!' and stood over him as if transfixed.

"Anything approaching the change that came over his features I have never seen before, and hope never to see again. Oh, I wasn't touched. I was fascinated. It was as though a veil had been

rent. I saw on that ivory face the expression of
sombre pride, of ruthless power, of craven terror—
of an intense and hopeless despair. Did he live
his life again in every detail of desire, temptation,
and surrender during that supreme moment of
complete knowledge? He cried in a whisper at
some image, at some vision—he cried out twice, a
cry that was no more than a breath:

"'The horror! The horror!'

"I blew the candle out and left the cabin. The
pilgrims were dining in the mess-room, and I
took my place opposite the manager, who lifted
his eyes to give me a questioning glance, which I
successfully ignored. He leaned back, serene, with
that peculiar smile of his sealing the unexpressed
depths of his meanness. A continuous shower
of small flies streamed upon the lamp, upon the
cloth, upon our hands and faces. Suddenly the
manager's boy put his insolent black head in the
doorway, and said in a tone of scathing contempt:

"'Mistah Kurtz—he dead.'

"All the pilgrims rushed out to see. I remained,
and went on with my dinner. I believe I was
considered brutally callous. However, I did not eat
much. There was a lamp in there—light, don't you
know—and outside it was so beastly, beastly dark.
I went no more near the remarkable man who had

pronounced a judgment upon the adventures of
his soul on this earth. The voice was gone. What
else had been there? But I am of course aware
that next day the pilgrims buried something in a
muddy hole.

"And then they very nearly buried me.

"However, as you see, I did not go to join Kurtz
there and then. I did not. I remained to dream
the nightmare out to the end, and to show my
loyalty to Kurtz once more. Destiny. My destiny!
Droll thing life is—that mysterious arrangement
of merciless logic for a futile purpose. The
most you can hope from it is some knowledge
of yourself—that comes too late—a crop of
unextinguishable regrets. I have wrestled with
death. It is the most unexciting contest you can
imagine. It takes place in an impalpable greyness,
with nothing underfoot, with nothing around,
without spectators, without clamour, without
glory, without the great desire of victory, without
the great fear of defeat, in a sickly atmosphere of
tepid scepticism, without much belief in your own
right, and still less in that of your adversary. If
such is the form of ultimate wisdom, then life is a
greater riddle than some of us think it to be. I was
within a hair's breadth of the last opportunity for
pronouncement, and I found with humiliation that

probably I would have nothing to say. This is the
reason why I affirm that Kurtz was a remarkable
man. He had something to say. He said it. Since
I had peeped over the edge myself, I understand
better the meaning of his stare, that could not see
the flame of the candle, but was wide enough to
embrace the whole universe, piercing enough to
penetrate all the hearts that beat in the darkness.
He had summed up—he had judged. 'The horror!'
He was a remarkable man. After all, this was the
expression of some sort of belief; it had candour, it
had conviction, it had a vibrating note of revolt in
its whisper, it had the appalling face of a glimpsed
truth—the strange commingling of desire and hate.
And it is not my own extremity I remember best—a
vision of greyness without form filled with physical
pain, and a careless contempt for the evanescence
of all things—even of this pain itself. No! It is his
extremity that I seem to have lived through. True,
he had made that last stride, he had stepped over
the edge, while I had been permitted to draw back
my hesitating foot. And perhaps in this is the
whole difference; perhaps all the wisdom, and all
truth, and all sincerity, are just compressed into
that inappreciable moment of time in which we
step over the threshold of the invisible. Perhaps! I
like to think my summing-up would not have been

a word of careless contempt. Better his cry—much better. It was an affirmation, a moral victory paid for by innumerable defeats, by abominable terrors, by abominable satisfactions. But it was a victory! That is why I have remained loyal to Kurtz to the last, and even beyond, when a long time after I heard once more, not his own voice, but the echo of his magnificent eloquence thrown to me from a soul as translucently pure as a cliff of crystal.

"No, they did not bury me, though there is a period of time which I remember mistily, with a shuddering wonder, like a passage through some inconceivable world that had no hope in it and no desire. I found myself back in the sepulchral city resenting the sight of people hurrying through the streets to filch a little money from each other, to devour their infamous cookery, to gulp their unwholesome beer, to dream their insignificant and silly dreams. They trespassed upon my thoughts. They were intruders whose knowledge of life was to me an irritating pretence, because I felt so sure they could not possibly know the things I knew. Their bearing, which was simply the bearing of commonplace individuals going about their business in the assurance of perfect safety, was offensive to me like the outrageous flauntings of folly in the face of a danger it is

unable to comprehend. I had no particular desire
to enlighten them, but I had some difficulty in
restraining myself from laughing in their faces
so full of stupid importance. I daresay I was
not very well at that time. I tottered about the
streets—there were various affairs to settle—
grinning bitterly at perfectly respectable persons.
I admit my behaviour was inexcusable, but then
my temperature was seldom normal in these
days. My dear aunt's endeavours to 'nurse up
my strength' seemed altogether beside the mark.
It was not my strength that wanted nursing,
it was my imagination that wanted soothing. I
kept the bundle of papers given me by Kurtz, not
knowing exactly what to do with it. His mother
had died lately, watched over, as I was told, by
his Intended. A clean-shaved man, with an official
manner and wearing gold-rimmed spectacles,
called on me one day and made inquiries, at first
circuitous, afterwards suavely pressing, about
what he was pleased to denominate certain
'documents.' I was not surprised, because I had
had two rows with the manager on the subject
out there. I had refused to give up the smallest
scrap out of that package, and I took the same
attitude with the spectacled man. He became
darkly menacing at last, and with much heat

argued that the Company had the right to every bit of information about its 'territories.' And said he, 'Mr. Kurtz's knowledge of unexplored regions must have been necessarily extensive and peculiar—owing to his great abilities and to the deplorable circumstances in which he had been placed: therefore—' I assured him Mr. Kurtz's knowledge, however extensive, did not bear upon the problems of commerce or administration. He invoked then the name of science. 'It would be an incalculable loss if,' etc., etc. I offered him the report on the 'Suppression of Savage Customs,' with the postscriptum torn off. He took it up eagerly, but ended by sniffing at it with an air of contempt. 'This is not what we had a right to expect,' he remarked. 'Expect nothing else,' I said. 'There are only private letters.' He withdrew upon some threat of legal proceedings, and I saw him no more; but another fellow, calling himself Kurtz's cousin, appeared two days later, and was anxious to hear all the details about his dear relative's last moments. Incidentally he gave me to understand that Kurtz had been essentially a great musician. 'There was the making of an immense success,' said the man, who was an organist, I believe, with lank grey hair flowing over a greasy coat-collar. I had no reason to doubt his statement; and to

this day I am unable to say what was Kurtz's
profession, whether he ever had any—which was
the greatest of his talents. I had taken him for
a painter who wrote for the papers, or else for a
journalist who could paint—but even the cousin
(who took snuff during the interview) could not
tell me what he had been—exactly. He was a
universal genius—on that point I agreed with the
old chap, who thereupon blew his nose noisily
into a large cotton handkerchief and withdrew in
senile agitation, bearing off some family letters
and memoranda without importance. Ultimately
a journalist anxious to know something of the
fate of his 'dear colleague' turned up. This visitor
informed me Kurtz's proper sphere ought to have
been politics 'on the popular side.' He had furry
straight eyebrows, bristly hair cropped short,
an eyeglass on a broad ribbon, and, becoming
expansive, confessed his opinion that Kurtz really
couldn't write a bit—'but heavens! how that man
could talk. He electrified large meetings. He had
faith—don't you see?—he had the faith. He could
get himself to believe anything—anything. He
would have been a splendid leader of an extreme
party.' 'What party?' I asked. 'Any party,' answered
the other. 'He was an—an—extremist.' Did I not
think so? I assented. Did I know, he asked, with

a sudden flash of curiosity, 'what it was that
had induced him to go out there?' 'Yes,' said I,
and forthwith handed him the famous Report for
publication, if he thought fit. He glanced through
it hurriedly, mumbling all the time, judged 'it
would do,' and took himself off with this plunder.

"Thus I was left at last with a slim packet of
letters and the girl's portrait. She struck me as
beautiful—I mean she had a beautiful expression.
I know that the sunlight can be made to lie, too,
yet one felt that no manipulation of light and
pose could have conveyed the delicate shade of
truthfulness upon those features. She seemed
ready to listen without mental reservation, without
suspicion, without a thought for herself. I concluded
I would go and give her back her portrait and
those letters myself. Curiosity? Yes; and also some
other feeling perhaps. All that had been Kurtz's
had passed out of my hands: his soul, his body,
his station, his plans, his ivory, his career. There
remained only his memory and his Intended—and I
wanted to give that up, too, to the past, in a way—to
surrender personally all that remained of him with
me to that oblivion which is the last word of our
common fate. I don't defend myself. I had no clear
perception of what it was I really wanted. Perhaps
it was an impulse of unconscious loyalty, or the

fulfilment of one of those ironic necessities that lurk in the facts of human existence. I don't know. I can't tell. But I went.

"I thought his memory was like the other memories of the dead that accumulate in every man's life—a vague impress on the brain of shadows that had fallen on it in their swift and final passage; but before the high and ponderous door, between the tall houses of a street as still and decorous as a well-kept alley in a cemetery, I had a vision of him on the stretcher, opening his mouth voraciously, as if to devour all the earth with all its mankind. He lived then before me; he lived as much as he had ever lived—a shadow insatiable of splendid appearances, of frightful realities; a shadow darker than the shadow of the night, and draped nobly in the folds of a gorgeous eloquence. The vision seemed to enter the house with me—the stretcher, the phantom-bearers, the wild crowd of obedient worshippers, the gloom of the forests, the glitter of the reach between the murky bends, the beat of the drum, regular and muffled like the beating of a heart—the heart of a conquering darkness. It was a moment of triumph for the wilderness, an invading and vengeful rush which, it seemed to me, I would have to keep back alone for the salvation of another soul. And the

memory of what I had heard him say afar there,
with the horned shapes stirring at my back, in
the glow of fires, within the patient woods, those
broken phrases came back to me, were heard
again in their ominous and terrifying simplicity.
I remembered his abject pleading, his abject
threats, the colossal scale of his vile desires,
the meanness, the torment, the tempestuous
anguish of his soul. And later on I seemed to
see his collected languid manner, when he said
one day, 'This lot of ivory now is really mine. The
Company did not pay for it. I collected it myself at
a very great personal risk. I am afraid they will try
to claim it as theirs though. H'm. It is a difficult
case. What do you think I ought to do—resist?
Eh? I want no more than justice.' . . . He wanted
no more than justice—no more than justice. I
rang the bell before a mahogany door on the first
floor, and while I waited he seemed to stare at me
out of the glassy panel—stare with that wide and
immense stare embracing, condemning, loathing
all the universe. I seemed to hear the whispered
cry, "The horror! The horror!"

"The dusk was falling. I had to wait in a lofty
drawing-room with three long windows from
floor to ceiling that were like three luminous and
bedraped columns. The bent gilt legs and backs

of the furniture shone in indistinct curves. The
tall marble fireplace had a cold and monumental
whiteness. A grand piano stood massively in a
corner; with dark gleams on the flat surfaces like
a sombre and polished sarcophagus. A high door
opened—closed. I rose.

"She came forward, all in black, with a pale
head, floating towards me in the dusk. She was
in mourning. It was more than a year since his
death, more than a year since the news came;
she seemed as though she would remember and
mourn forever. She took both my hands in hers
and murmured, 'I had heard you were coming.'
I noticed she was not very young—I mean not
girlish. She had a mature capacity for fidelity,
for belief, for suffering. The room seemed to have
grown darker, as if all the sad light of the cloudy
evening had taken refuge on her forehead. This
fair hair, this pale visage, this pure brow, seemed
surrounded by an ashy halo from which the dark
eyes looked out at me. Their glance was guileless,
profound, confident, and trustful. She carried
her sorrowful head as though she were proud of
that sorrow, as though she would say, 'I—I alone
know how to mourn for him as he deserves.' But
while we were still shaking hands, such a look
of awful desolation came upon her face that I

perceived she was one of those creatures that are not the playthings of Time. For her he had died only yesterday. And, by Jove! the impression was so powerful that for me, too, he seemed to have died only yesterday—nay, this very minute. I saw her and him in the same instant of time—his death and her sorrow—I saw her sorrow in the very moment of his death. Do you understand? I saw them together—I heard them together. She had said, with a deep catch of the breath, 'I have survived' while my strained ears seemed to hear distinctly, mingled with her tone of despairing regret, the summing up whisper of his eternal condemnation. I asked myself what I was doing there, with a sensation of panic in my heart as though I had blundered into a place of cruel and absurd mysteries not fit for a human being to behold. She motioned me to a chair. We sat down. I laid the packet gently on the little table, and she put her hand over it. . . . 'You knew him well,' she murmured, after a moment of mourning silence.

"'Intimacy grows quick out there,' I said. 'I knew him as well as it is possible for one man to know another.'

"'And you admired him,' she said. 'It was impossible to know him and not to admire him. Was it?'

"'He was a remarkable man,' I said, unsteadily. Then before the appealing fixity of her gaze, that seemed to watch for more words on my lips, I went on, 'It was impossible not to—'

"'Love him,' she finished eagerly, silencing me into an appalled dumbness. 'How true! how true! But when you think that no one knew him so well as I! I had all his noble confidence. I knew him best.'

"'You knew him best,' I repeated. And perhaps she did. But with every word spoken the room was growing darker, and only her forehead, smooth and white, remained illumined by the inextinguishable light of belief and love.

"'You were his friend,' she went on. 'His friend,' she repeated, a little louder. 'You must have been, if he had given you this, and sent you to me. I feel I can speak to you—and oh! I must speak. I want you—you who have heard his last words—to know I have been worthy of him. . . . It is not pride. . . . Yes! I am proud to know I understood him better than any one on earth—he told me so himself. And since his mother died I have had no one—no one—to—to—'

"I listened. The darkness deepened. I was not even sure whether he had given me the right bundle. I rather suspect he wanted me to take

care of another batch of his papers, which, after
his death, I saw the manager examining under the
lamp. And the girl talked, easing her pain in the
certitude of my sympathy; she talked as thirsty
men drink. I had heard that her engagement with
Kurtz had been disapproved by her people. He
wasn't rich enough or something. And indeed I
don't know whether he had not been a pauper all
his life. He had given me some reason to infer that
it was his impatience of comparative poverty that
drove him out there.

"'. . . Who was not his friend who had heard
him speak once?' she was saying. 'He drew men
towards him by what was best in them.' She
looked at me with intensity. 'It is the gift of the
great,' she went on, and the sound of her low
voice seemed to have the accompaniment of all
the other sounds, full of mystery, desolation,
and sorrow, I had ever heard—the ripple of the
river, the soughing of the trees swayed by the
wind, the murmurs of the crowds, the faint ring
of incomprehensible words cried from afar, the
whisper of a voice speaking from beyond the
threshold of an eternal darkness. 'But you have
heard him! You know!' she cried.

"'Yes, I know,' I said with something like despair
in my heart, but bowing my head before the faith

that was in her, before that great and saving
illusion that shone with an unearthly glow in the
darkness, in the triumphant darkness from which
I could not have defended her—from which I could
not even defend myself.

"'What a loss to me—to us!'—she corrected
herself with beautiful generosity; then added in
a murmur, 'To the world.' By the last gleams of
twilight I could see the glitter of her eyes, full of
tears—of tears that would not fall.

"'I have been very happy—very fortunate—very
proud,' she went on. 'Too fortunate. Too happy for
a little while. And now I am unhappy for—for life.'

"She stood up; her fair hair seemed to catch
all the remaining light in a glimmer of gold. I rose,
too.

"'And of all this,' she went on mournfully,
'of all his promise, and of all his greatness, of
his generous mind, of his noble heart, nothing
remains—nothing but a memory. You and I—'

"'We shall always remember him,' I said hastily.

"'No!' she cried. 'It is impossible that all
this should be lost—that such a life should be
sacrificed to leave nothing—but sorrow. You know
what vast plans he had. I knew of them, too—I
could not perhaps understand—but others knew

of them. Something must remain. His words, at least, have not died.'

"'His words will remain,' I said.

"'And his example,' she whispered to herself. 'Men looked up to him—his goodness shone in every act. His example—'

"'True,' I said; 'his example, too. Yes, his example. I forgot that.'

"'But I do not. I cannot—I cannot believe—not yet. I cannot believe that I shall never see him again, that nobody will see him again, never, never, never.'

"She put out her arms as if after a retreating figure, stretching them back and with clasped pale hands across the fading and narrow sheen of the window. Never see him! I saw him clearly enough then. I shall see this eloquent phantom as long as I live, and I shall see her, too, a tragic and familiar Shade, resembling in this gesture another one, tragic also, and bedecked with powerless charms, stretching bare brown arms over the glitter of the infernal stream, the stream of darkness. She said suddenly very low, 'He died as he lived.'

"'His end,' said I, with dull anger stirring in me, 'was in every way worthy of his life.'

"'And I was not with him,' she murmured. My anger subsided before a feeling of infinite pity.

"'Everything that could be done—' I mumbled.

"'Ah, but I believed in him more than any one on earth—more than his own mother, more than—himself. He needed me! Me! I would have treasured every sigh, every word, every sign, every glance.'

"I felt like a chill grip on my chest. 'Don't,' I said, in a muffled voice.

"'Forgive me. I—I have mourned so long in silence—in silence. . . . You were with him—to the last? I think of his loneliness. Nobody near to understand him as I would have understood. Perhaps no one to hear. . . .'

"'To the very end,' I said, shakily. 'I heard his very last words. . . .' I stopped in a fright.

"'Repeat them,' she murmured in a heart-broken tone. 'I want—I want—something—something—to—to live with.'

"I was on the point of crying at her, 'Don't you hear them?' The dusk was repeating them in a persistent whisper all around us, in a whisper that seemed to swell menacingly like the first whisper of a rising wind. 'The horror! The horror!'

"'His last word—to live with,' she insisted. 'Don't you understand I loved him—I loved him—I loved him!'

"I pulled myself together and spoke slowly.

"'The last word he pronounced was—your name.'

"I heard a light sigh and then my heart stood still, stopped dead short by an exulting and terrible cry, by the cry of inconceivable triumph and of unspeakable pain. 'I knew it—I was sure!'. . . She knew. She was sure. I heard her weeping; she had hidden her face in her hands. It seemed to me that the house would collapse before I could escape, that the heavens would fall upon my head. But nothing happened. The heavens do not fall for such a trifle. Would they have fallen, I wonder, if I had rendered Kurtz that justice which was his due? Hadn't he said he wanted only justice? But I couldn't. I could not tell her. It would have been too dark—too dark altogether. . . ."

Marlow ceased, and sat apart, indistinct and silent, in the pose of a meditating Buddha. Nobody moved for a time. "We have lost the first of the ebb," said the Director suddenly. I raised my head. The offing was barred by a black bank of clouds, and the tranquil waterway leading to the uttermost ends of the earth flowed sombre under an overcast sky—seemed to lead into the heart of an immense darkness.

PART 3
REFLECTION QUESTIONS

1. How is the absurdity of the Russian further developed by Marlow's impression and description of him? Later in the reading, consider how the Russian serves as a foil and/or a doppelganger (double or alter ego) to Kurtz.

2. Why does Marlow say of the Russian (whom he later describes as Kurtz's "last disciple"), "I did not envy him his devotion to Kurtz, though.

He had not meditated over it. It came to him, and he accepted it with a sort of eager fatalism."

3. Why does the Russian tell Marlow, "You can't judge Mr. Kurtz as you would an ordinary man"?

4. What does Marlow mean when he relays that Kurtz's months-long absence from his station was spent "getting himself adored"? Why does Marlow characterize this as one of Kurtz's "less material aspirations"?

5. What does Marlow realize about the ornamentation placed outside Kurtz's compound? What do the heads symbolize, particularly the fact that their faces are turned towards Kurtz's dwelling?

6. Marlowe says that "Kurtz lacked restraint in the gratification of his various lusts." When is mere restraint of a sinful desire enough? When is it not? How does 2 Timothy 2:22 address this question?

7. What does the manager's statement that Kurtz's "methods had ruined the district" mean? How is the preoccupation with "method" throughout the story reflect on the values of Conrad's culture?

8. What do Marlow's words in this passage reveal about himself, Kurtz, and the imperialistic European society they reflect? "I want you clearly to understand that there was nothing exactly profitable in these heads being there. They only showed that Mr. Kurtz lacked restraint in the gratification of his various lusts, that there was something wanting in him—some small matter which, when the pressing need arose, could not be found under his magnificent eloquence. Whether he knew of this deficiency himself I can't say. I think the knowledge came to him at last—only at the very last. But the wilderness had found him out early, and had taken on him a terrible vengeance for the fantastic invasion. I think it had whispered to him things about himself which he did not know, things of which he had no conception till he took counsel with this great solitude—and the whisper had proved irresistibly fascinating. It echoed loudly within him because he was hollow at the core. . . ."

9. What role does the Russian have in revealing more to Marlow about Kurtz? What is the effect of Conrad's artistic choice to reveal the crucial information about Kurtz in this way and at this place in the story?

10. What does Marlow say he does not want to know about Kurtz? Why do you think he does not want to know?

11. Describe how Kurtz appears when Marlow sees him for the first time. How do his condition and behavior compare to all that has been revealed about him up to this point in the story?

12. Marlow refers to Kurtz several times as "a voice." What is the significance of this?

13. After taking Kurtz in, Marlow encounters "a wild and gorgeous apparition of a woman." Does she seem like a realistic character or one drawn from stereotype? Why is her role significant in the story?

14. In his discussion with the manager about Kurtz's "unsound methods," Marlow defends Kurtz. Then, Marlow says, "My hour of favour was over; I found myself lumped along with Kurtz as a partisan of methods for which the time was not ripe: I was unsound! Ah! but it was something to have at least a choice of nightmares." What in the world of this story makes having "a choice of nightmares" so important? (Consider the rising

influence of existentialism, discussed in the introduction.) Pay attention throughout to the imagery in the story that evokes the mood and feelings of a nightmare.

15. What does Marlow mean by these words about Kurtz? "No eloquence could have been so withering to one's belief in mankind as his final burst of sincerity. He struggled with himself, too. I saw it—I heard it. I saw the inconceivable mystery of a soul that knew no restraint, no faith, and no fear, yet struggling blindly with itself."

16. Much of what Kurtz has done and become is described in cloaked, enigmatic language, such as when Marlow says that "Mr. Kurtz's adorers were keeping their uneasy vigil" and earlier when Marlow interrupts the Russian as he describes the natives crawling during the "the ceremonies used when approaching Kurtz." What is the relationship between Kurtz and the natives implied, and what effect does the use of this muted language have on the reader's growing understanding of what has happened to Kurtz?

17. What does Kurtz's escape and the manner of it further reveal about his physical, mental, and spiritual condition?

18. The exact title phrase appears twice in the work, first in Part 1: "We penetrated deeper and deeper into the heart of darkness. It was very quiet there. At night sometimes the roll of drums behind the curtain of trees would run up the river and remain sustained faintly, as if hovering in the air high over our heads, till the first break of day. Whether it meant war, peace, or prayer we could not tell." It appears again in Part 3: "The brown current ran swiftly out of the heart of darkness, bearing us down towards the sea with twice the speed of our upward progress; and Kurtz's life was running swiftly, too, ebbing, ebbing out of his heart into the sea of inexorable time." What does the phrase mean? How do context and imagery add to its possible meanings?

19. The death of Kurtz and his last words are the most famous part of the book: "Anything approaching the change that came over his fea-tures I have never seen before, and hope never to see again. Oh, I wasn't touched. I was fascinated. It was as though a veil had been rent. I saw on

that ivory face the expression of sombre pride, of ruthless power, of craven terror—of an intense and hopeless despair. Did he live his life again in every detail of desire, temptation, and surrender during that supreme moment of complete knowledge? He cried in a whisper at some image, at some vision— he cried out twice, a cry that was no more than a breath: "'The horror! The horror!'" What might Kurtz's final words mean?

20. Marlow says that in his death, Kurtz seems to have "glimpsed truth." Then Marlow says, "It is his extremity that I seem to have lived through. True, he had made that last stride, he had stepped over the edge, while I had been permitted to draw back my hesitating foot." What does this mean?

21. Immediately following Kurtz's death comes this famous line (one used as an epigraph in T. S. Eliot's poem, "The Hollow Men"): Suddenly the manager's boy put his insolent black head in the doorway, and said in a tone of scathing contempt: "'Mistah Kurtz—he dead.'" What is the effect of this anti-climactic report of Kurtz's death?

22. Marlow says that Kurtz's last words—"The horror!"—were "the expression of some sort of belief." What does Marlow mean by this?

23. When Marlow turns in Kurtz's report, "The Suppression of Savage Customs," he says he did so with the "postscriptum torn off." Recall that in the postscript, Kurtz had scrawled, "Exterminate all the brutes!" What does it say about Marlow that he withholds this from the company?

24. What is the meaning of this exchange Marlow has with a company official: "He electrified large meetings. He had faith—don't you see?—he had the faith. He could get himself to believe anything—anything. He would have been a splendid leader of an extreme party.' 'What party?' I asked. 'Any party,' answered the other. 'He was an—an—extremist'"?

25. How is Kurtz's Intended linked to the theme of truth in both her description and in Marlow's actions concerning her?

26. In Part 1, Marlow says he "can't bear a lie . . . There is a taint of death, a flavour of mortality in lies." How then do you explain the lie he tells

Kurtz's Intended? How does Marlow justify his lie to Kurtz's fiancée?

27. How would you characterize Marlow's relationship to Kurtz? Why does Marlow feel drawn to and protective of Kurtz? Is Kurtz his alter ego? Does Marlow worship Kurtz like the natives did?

28. Marlow and Kurtz are the only two characters who are named. What other parallels can be seen between them?

29. Is Marlow a static character or a dynamic one? In other words, does he remain the same from the start of his story or does he change?

30. The last few lines of the narrative return to the frame around the central story—the men sitting in the darkness on a boat listening to Marlow's tale. What is the significance of the last sentence and its closing image?

FOR FURTHER REFLECTION

1. How does the overall story change because of the device of the frame narrative? In other words, how would the story be different if it consisted only of Marlow's narration without the setting in which it occurs and the presence of the actual narrator?

2. How does the three-part structure of the narrative contribute to the meaning and effect of the story?

3. What makes *Heart of Darkness* a difficult read?

4. Do you find Conrad's dense, image-laden language to be poetic and lyrical? Or do you agree more with Chinua Achebe's judgment that Conrad merely achieves a "hypnotic stupor in his readers through a bombardment of emotive words"?

5. What are the most repeated words, phrases, and images in the work? How do these refrains contribute to the overall meaning and effect of the story?

6. Do the racist elements of the novella overwhelm its other qualities? Why or why not? Discuss this question with readers of different racial and ethnic backgrounds for further insights on this question.

7. Why does Marlow focus on Kurtz's eloquence? What role does eloquence have in Kurtz's story and in his own story? What are the strengths and limitations of eloquence? What does the Bible say about eloquence? (See, for example, Exodus 4:10–16, Proverbs 7:21, Acts 18:24, 1 Corinthians 1:17, 1 Corinthians 2:1–5, 2 Corinthians 10:10, 2 Corinthians 11:6, and Colossians 4:6.)

8. Does the story seem tied to a particular time and place in history or does it transcend these to address more universal, timeless concerns?

9. How is idolatry at work in the novel? Not only the idolatry of Kurtz (by the Russian, by the natives, and possibly by Marlow), but other kinds of idolatries as well?

10. Besides idolatry, what other sins are at the root of the events in the story?

11. A symbol is something that has both a literal meaning or function and at the same time stands for something else, such as an idea or concept. Symbols in *Heart of Darkness* include ivory, drums, the Russian harlequin, and, of course, darkness. What are the literal and symbolic functions of these elements of the story?

12. The narrative begins and closes with the image of the offing, that is, the deep part of the sea visible from the shore. Literally, the offing is part of the setting. Is it also symbolic? What does it suggest?

13. Despite the darkness that pervades the story, are there any hints of redemption or hope?

14. What passages might a postmodern reading of the text—one that seeks to undermine belief in absolute certainty or a trustworthy narrative—emphasize? How does a biblical understanding of both human fallibility and divine, absolute Truth answer such a reading? How does the story itself support or fail to support this biblical understanding?

15. Can an attentive and faithful reading of a work like this help the Christian to follow Paul's exhortation in Philippians 4:8? How so?

EXPLORE
the CLASSICS
with other books from this series

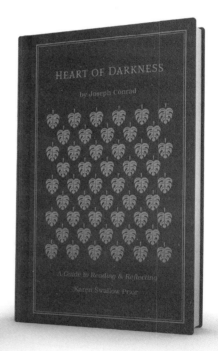

ADDITIONAL TITLES
FORTHCOMING:

Frankenstein by Mary Shelley
Jane Eyre by Charlotte Bronte